Chapter 1

Topher found the cat in the shed at the bottom of the garden. It was on a pile of old newspapers. He'd just come home from school and had gone to the shed to look for a coupon for a free offer he'd missed. He was into free offers. This one was for snuff, whatever that was. 'Snuff it and see,' the advert had said. Anyway, he'd found the papers easily because his dad was a tidiness fanatic – and there in a box labelled OLD NEWSPAPERS was the cat, curled up like a Chelsea bun. The spiralling lines of her sleeping body had a golden glow, and the gold was flecked with black and white like currants and sugar. She was beautiful, the most beautiful cat he had ever seen, and yet strangely she seemed familiar. She had tabby markings but she wasn't mostly grey like ordinary tabbies. She wasn't an ordinary anything. He should have known that from the start.

Right now he simply bent down to stroke her – it was odd how he was sure she was a she – and he forgot the snuff, the newspapers, everything.

'You're very thin, puss.'

She opened an amber eye. It was like a warning light.

'Your ears are enormous.'

And her tail seemed too long for her body.

'Mwa!'

3

It was a loud cry for a small cat, more a wail than a mew. He scratched between her ears and she stood up, stretched, arched, her tail like an exclamation mark.

'Mwa! Mwaa!' Both eyes were open now – and her mouth.

'Are you hungry, cat? Stay here then. I'll get you some milk.'

He closed the shed door, though he was sure she would have followed him, but he wasn't sure what his dad would say. He'd be home shortly.

Six months ago he wouldn't have noticed whether there was a cat in the house or not, but he'd changed. Everything had changed. His dad used to be a real absent-minded professor. He worked at the university. Now he seemed to want to control everything. You only had to look at the weedless border by the path, at the dead daffodils all tied up in neat bundles, and the pruned rose bushes. Didn't cats dig in gardens?

There wasn't any milk in the fridge, so he had to get it from the front step. Sunlight shone through the stained glass in the door, throwing coloured patterns on the black and white tiles. Outside, a dog was peeing against a plane tree, deepening the yellow of the patchy bark and little kids were racing past on trikes. It would be nice to have a cat, better than coming home to an empty house. Over the road a pigeon cooed from a chimney pot shaped like a tall crown. They were old-fashioned terraced houses in Arburton Road. Topher liked the higgledy-piggledy roof line.

'Hi.' It was Lisa from Number 47.

He closed the door smartish. Lisa was like a Barbie doll.

4

Back in the kitchen, he carefully filled a saucer, and carried it down the garden path to the shed.

For a miserable second he thought the cat wasn't there. Then she leaped from a shelf to greet him, purred ecstatically as she rubbed around his legs. He put the milk on the floor and she lapped hungrily, splashing it over the edge.

And he longed for her to be his.

'Where have you come from, cat? You are a stray, aren't you?'

He couldn't bear her to belong to anyone else. She had to be his.

Then suddenly he changed his mind. Remembered. The sadness was back, like a stone in his throat.

'Shoo, cat!' He opened the door.

She looked at him, her eyes round with astonishment. There was a little beard of milk on her chin.

'Shoo!' He waved his arms.

'Mwow.' She wound round his legs.

I'm yours, Topher, yours.

He had to laugh at himself, imagining her speaking to him.

'Oh, no you're not. Scat cat!'

'Mwow-ow.'

I'm yours, Topher, yours.

He wished he hadn't given her the milk. There was no point in getting attached.

'Skedaddle!' He clapped his hands. She must go, now.

But she wouldn't go. She sat down and started to wash the tip of her tail. So he picked her up and plonked her outside the shed, closed the door.

Then he ran back to the house, remembered there

5

was a lot of post and it was all for him. He'd sent for some things from a book called *Free Stuff*. It was a bit of a swiz because only a few things were free, just a leaflet about sign language for talking to the deaf, and another one about a language called Esperanto. These had come and so had some postcards of a dinosaur called Claws. He'd had to pay for the postcards, but they were really worth it. The dinosaur had only just been discovered, in Surrey, not far away really. It had been in a clay pit for 124 million years, till a man who worked there found it. Imagine that, finding a dinosaur. He was trying to when he heard the front door go. He looked at his watch.

6.15 exactly. It had to be his dad.

Topher timed him.

Fifteen seconds to hang up his suit jacket on the hall stand and look in the mirror. Ten seconds to loosen his tie. Five seconds to see if there was any post and three to stride up the hall. Then he was in the kitchen doorway, rolling up his sleeves.

'Hello, Topher. Good day? Ah, there's the post. Anything for me?'

Topher shook his head.

Sometimes their letters got muddled. It was having the same name that did it, Christopher Hope. His dad was called Chris and he was called Topher, but that didn't usually help with letters. The same but different names had been his mum's idea.

But Topher didn't want to think of her.

He was training himself not to.

Now his dad was putting on a plastic apron. It had pigs on and it didn't suit him. He was a tall serious-looking man with dark-rimmed glasses. He was peering through them at a list on the wall.

'Now what's for the trough today?'

Making jokes didn't suit him either.

'Ah. Tuesday. Spaghetti Bolognese.' He got some mince from the fridge.

Tuesday – spaghetti.

Wednesday – chops.

And so on, every week the same.

'We've got to have a system, son. Then we can cope.' He said it every day. 'Your mum would have wanted us to.'

And every day Topher wanted to shout, 'How do you know?'

But he didn't. He changed the subject instead, told his dad about Claws.

'It's in the Natural History Museum. It was a flesh eater.'

'Let's have a look then.'

Topher held out one of the postcards.

His dad was chopping onions. 'We can go and see it on Sunday if you like.'

'Great.'

Later they ate in silence. Topher read about Baronyx Walkeri, which was the dinosaur's proper name; it had been named after the Mr Walker who had found it, and his dad read the *Evening Standard*.

It was while they were doing the washing-up that the cat reappeared – on the kitchen window-sill. His dad saw it first.

'Blimey.' He never swore properly.

'What?'

7

'That cat, it's the spitting image.'

She wasn't spitting. She was staring through the window – at Topher.

'She's the double I mean, of that carving your mother gave you. She's even got the ankh on her forehead. You know, the Egyptian sign of life.'

That was it. That's why she'd seemed familiar. Topher carried on drying.

'Where is it, by the way? The carving I mean.' His dad was drying his hands.

It was in the cupboard by the side of his bed. Out of sight. His mum had brought it back from Memphis. She'd been an Egyptologist, an expert on Ancient Egypt.

The cat was yowling now. His dad opened the window.

'You're in luck, cat. There's a bit of mince left.'

'Don't encourage it!' Topher surprised himself. This is what he'd expected his dad to say.

'Why not? If it's a stray you could keep it.'

'I don't want it.'

But his dad didn't seem to hear, was already scraping mince into a margarine container, and the cat was nudging his hand trying to start eating.

'You could call her Ka. That's Egyptian for a double. Amazing. I'd never have believed a real cat could look so much like a lump of stone. Onyx, isn't it, the carving?'

'Sardonyx. Onyx is black and white.'

The Egyptian cat was black and white and reddish gold, and the cat spattering sauce on the kitchen floor looked amazingly like it.

'I've been thinking, Topher, a pet, it would take you

8

out of yourself.' Topher went outside. It was a stupid phrase. He'd heard it too many times before. Do this, Topher, do that. It'll take you out of yourself. He imagined himself stepping out of his skin, leaving his body behind. Sometimes he wished he could.

He stayed in the garden till he saw his dad leave the kitchen then went back. The cat was still there. He could hear her purring. She was on a chair half under the table. He tipped it up and she clung to the rushwork seat, spat, hissed. He shook the chair and still she clung on, shredding the rushes with her claws.

'Scat cat!' He shook the chair again and eventually dislodged her. Then he heaved her out of the door.

'I said GO!' He slammed the door. Then he examined the scratches on his hands while watching her from the window. He could still see his fingermarks in her fur as she strolled to the middle of the lawn. She sat down with her back to him, washed and smoothed herself, erasing him. Later, she sprang onto the fence and into the neighbour's garden. She didn't look back.

'Goodbye, cat.'

It really was best that she went.

But when he went to bed, he retrieved her double from the back of his bedside cupboard. It was wrapped in a silk scarf. Flame coloured, it reminded him of his mum. It still had her musky scent – so he put it back. The stone cat and the real cat were amazingly alike, though the carving felt cold as it always had. His mum had bought his dad a sardonyx ashtray from the same trip – she'd forgotten he'd stopped smoking – and the ashtray was good for putting on your forehead if you had a headache. She had come back from that trip. It

9

was the next one when the plane had crashed.

By the light of the lamp the stone cat looked even more like the real one. It had the same large translucent ears, the same golden glow. When he switched out the light it still glowed. Strange how he'd never noticed that before. Must be phosphorus in it, or radium. Making himself think scientifically about things which shone in the dark, he managed to fall asleep. And in sleep he thought he heard a cat outside his window, a golden cat with a musky scent.

'Mwa! Mwaa!'

Let me in, Topher. Let me in.

No. Go away. Stop bothering me. He pulled the pillow over his head.

Chapter 2

Something woke him in the night. What was it? He was facing the wall where circles of light were moving from left to right, right to left. Back again. Was it moonlight behind the trees? Car headlights? Someone with a torch? His father perhaps, but why?

'Dad?'

No reply.

'Dad, is that you?'

Still no reply, yet he felt someone behind him. Someone or something compelled him to turn. So he did, and found himself looking at a cat with large eyes; they were like moons. He laughed. Of course. The carving. He remembered its glow as he went to sleep, and now it glowed more brightly, especially its eyes. They gleamed. But how had they made those patterns on the wall? The cat was still as a stone – was stone.

'Mwa!' *Touch me*.

No I don't want to.

'Mwa!' *Touch me!*

A talking cat! Voices in his head? This was ridiculous. He must be dreaming. Pinching himself awake he sat up, turned away from the cat. And there on the wall were the circles of light, moving again – from left to right. From right to left. Again and again. Hypnotising him. But the voice behind him was even more compelling.

'Mwa! MWA!' *Touch me, Topher. Touch me. I'm YOURS.*

Then he turned and touched her, touched *Ka*, and felt his fingers sink into fur.

Chapter 3

He must have cried out because at breakfast his dad said, 'Did you have a nightmare, son? I thought I heard you in the night.'

Fortunately he didn't want an answer; he was rushing round getting ready for work. And Topher remembered him coming into his bedroom, switching on the light – and he remembered the fur beneath his fingers turning back to stone. Had it been a nightmare? But the fur had felt so real.

With daylight and cornflakes reason prevailed. Wasn't it more likely that the stray cat had returned, that Ka had returned? That she had got inside his room and mingled with his dreams? But how, and where was she now? And wouldn't she have left some sign? Now Topher longed for her. Longed to feel her fur on his fingers. It was as if touching her had kindled something inside him, something he thought he'd lost for ever. He had to find her again.

Toast in hand he ran upstairs.

'Steady on, son.' His dad was coming down.

There must be something – a paw print perhaps.

The stone cat was beside his bed. Could the real cat have pushed the stone one aside, taken its place, sat in front of it on the little white table? If it had, it had left no sign, not so much as a hair.

This morning the stone cat seemed dull, lifeless, and he remembered the lights moving across the wall. Even a real cat's eyes didn't give out beams. But there was a mirror on the wall. Could that have reflected the cat's shining pupils? Had it moved its head from side to side? He needed to think but his father was calling.

'Topher!'

He ought to be going.

'Topher! It's half past eight!'

The sash window was open at the bottom, so she could have climbed in. Must have. There was a roof below the window, and the garden wall beyond that. It would have been easy.

'Topher! Don't forget to close your window.' The front door banged shut. His dad was afraid of break-ins; there had been a few lately. Nevertheless, Topher left the window open.

And he looked for the cat all the way to school. How could he have chased her away?

Archway was a busy built-up area, with houses as far as you could see. It was hard looking for a cat with so many people on the pavements, and pushchairs and dog poop – and he needed all his wits crossing the roads. But what really surprised him was how many cats there were. Dozens! Smooth ones, fluffy ones, gingers, tabbies, black with white socks, white with black socks and a scruffy white one with a pirate patch. In Cressida Road a black one crossed his path! Topher hoped it meant good luck. Ka, how he longed for her. How rotten he'd been. No wonder she had gone. Oh no. He forced himself to look at a dead one in the gutter. It wasn't Ka.

As he got nearer to school there seemed to be more dogs than cats, smart ones with smart owners in track suits. They were probably on their way to the disused railway line behind Stanhope Gardens. It was great there. He used to go a lot with his friends – when he still had friends. It seemed a long time ago. He and Dylan Barnes had seen a fox once – yes, and cats! That's where she'd be! There were lots of cats there; semi-wild they were. He'd go after school.

Then 'Ka!'

He thought he saw her behind a wall, but it was a little tortoiseshell. It came and rubbed against his legs, purred. It was nice but it wasn't Ka, and doubt came into his head – about finding her on the railway line. He just couldn't imagine her living rough, catching her own food. Ka was a demanding looked-after sort of cat. She had an *imperious* air. Ka, how the name had stuck.

He didn't really want to go to school, couldn't remember ever seeing a cat in St. Saviour's playground. They had more sense. But here he was now.

'Hi, Topher.' Hayley Smedley was swinging on the gate. Balls hurtled in all directions, bouncing off the rusty railings, till the whistle went and everything froze. Then Mr Westlake blew the whistle again and Topher joined 6C's straggling line.

'What happened to you then? I waited for ages.' It was Dylan. They sometimes met on the way to school.

'I was looking for my cat.'

'Didn't know you had a cat.'

'You missed a good game, Hope.' That was Titch Warren.

'Quiet there!'

15

They were supposed to walk in quietly. No problem, he didn't feel like talking.

After register Miss Crabb told them about a new girl. She was going to join 6C the following week. Ellie Wentworth was deaf, she said, but she had a hearing device which helped a bit. Her teachers would have to wear a special device too, to amplify their voices during lessons, and Ellie would have to sit near the front. They would all have to listen carefully and speak clearly. Topher thought about the free leaflet he'd sent for – wondered if she knew sign language – but mostly he thought about Ka. He couldn't see out, the windows were too high, but he couldn't stop thinking about her. Dylan got really narky in Design and Technology. They were supposed to be designing a vehicle together, using an egg.

'I just asked you what we should make the axle out of, and do you know what you said?'

Topher had no idea.

'You said stone. Stone! I think you're stoned! I don't know what's the matter with you lately.' He went off to work on his own.

Topher didn't blame him. All he could think of was Ka. In Library they had to look up words in the dictionary. He went to look up 'Ka', but it wasn't in. Then he found a book about Ancient Egypt; he couldn't find it there either, but the book was interesting. The Egyptians were really weird. They thought dead people came alive again after they were buried, and that they carried on exactly as they had in their first lives. That's why they preserved their bodies as mummies and why they took all their things with them, even their pots and pans for cooking – and little statues of their servants who came alive and looked after them in the next life. Statues coming alive! It was barmy – and yet . . . He flicked over a few pages and there it was. Ka. The word seemed to jump out of the page.

'Ka.

Every living creature had a "Ka" or physical double which protected it during its life on earth. Sometimes it was a statue and they kept it in a special place.'

He copied it into his rough book. To confuse him even more, in science Dylan got Old Charlie on his favourite topic of relativity, Old Charlie's favourite topic that is. He went on and on about time and space, and his hero Albert Einstein. He said if you travelled millions of light years you would come back younger than when you went away. And he finished as he always did just as the bell went.

'So if Albert Einstein is right, boys and girls, last Wednesday *still exists*. Think about it.'

And Topher did. He thought about it as he walked along the overgrown railway line which he decided to search anyway. He thought about it as he walked home down Arburton Road, Ka-less. If last Wednesday still exists where is it? And what about all the other Wednesdays and the people who lived in them? Are they alive or dead? He thought about what the Egyptians thought, and he wondered if somewhere light years away they still existed. Mostly he thought about Ka.

She wasn't at home. She wasn't in the house or the garden. It seemed cold inside though the central heating

17

had come on. He went out into the street again and asked everyone he saw, describing her in detail, but nobody had seen a cat like Ka. He put a Lost Cat notice in the window of Angelo's Stores. Coming home he met his dad and asked him. He told him he'd changed his mind about keeping her. His dad said they could get another cat if Ka didn't turn up. Topher said he didn't want another cat. Later he asked his dad about relativity and time-travelling, but his answer didn't make sense. He said there was a book Topher could read when he was older. Feeling stupid and hopeless Topher went upstairs.

His bedroom window was still open. Pushing it up higher he leaned out and called again. Three doors away a woman was watering plants on her roof terrace. The ginger cat beside her looked up.

The stone cat was on the cupboard. What had happened last night? Had Ka really returned or had it all been a nightmare? That was an unbearable thought. To put it out of his mind he tried to read for a bit then switched off the light.

The stone cat didn't even glow.

But when he woke in the night it was gleaming.

Chapter 4

The cat was gleaming, and there was something else.

It was changing. Its stone surface was quickening. Like wind rippling a cornfield, something was breathing life into the cat. Already he could see the hair on its tail – on its back, its legs. The stone surface of the cat's body was changing – to *fur*! When claws appeared and the tip of its nose became pink skin, Topher thought the process was complete. Then whiskers sprang from the sides of its head.

'Ka!' He breathed it, almost laughing.

'Topher.' She was haughty, remembering no doubt how he had ejected her. Rejected her.

'I didn't mean it.'

He sat up.

She licked a paw.

'I want you to stay.'

He could see her clearly. The curtains were open and a full moon bathed her in light. She was even more beautiful than he remembered. On her forehead was a perfect ankh, in black tinged with gold. She was washing a leg now, bronze fur glistening.

'I want you to stay.'

She carried on washing.

'I'm sorry I sent you away.'

She was listening, he could tell. Her large ears twitched, the hairs inside them vibrating. She washed her other leg. Then looked straight at him.

'You want me to stay?'

Her voice was husky and precise.

'Yes.'

'Well, look at me.'

He had looked down when she looked up, thought he would drown in the black depths of her eyes. But now he looked into them, and was overcome. Wave after wave of light and dark flooded him.

Black amber.

Amber black.

He struggled to see her, struggled to say the words. The waves kept coming, drowning sight, drowning speech.

Light. Dark.

Dark. Light.

He fought back.

'I want you to stay.'

She blinked and the light went out. Then it flashed past him. Something landed on his feet. Ka! He felt the pull-prick of claws circling. Then she settled and slept and so did he.

Chapter 5

'So you've decided to keep her?' It was morning. His dad was by his bed with a tray. What was he talking about?

'The cat, she's come back I see. Hello, Ka.'

Topher felt fur against his feet. He sat up and saw Ka stretched at the bottom of his bed. His dad had two cups of tea. He must want to talk. Topher crawled to the end of the bed and buried his face in Ka's fur. Yes. His dad was going out with someone called Sylvia, he said. He'd mentioned her before, hadn't he? She worked in his office. They were going to play badminton.

'If that's all right with you, Topher?'

'Sure.'

'You don't mind then?'

''Course not.'

Just don't bring her here that's all. I don't want to look at her.

He didn't say that.

'You could come too, you know. There's a junior section.'

'No thanks.'

'We might go for a drink afterwards, then.'

'Fine.'

'Anyway I'll see you before I go. And I'll leave you money for some cat food. Don't forget your tea.' He put it on the bedside table.

When his dad had gone Topher spoke to the cat. She didn't answer him, just lay at the bottom of his bed. He stroked her till her fur rippled, talking, waiting. She purred, said nothing. But when he went downstairs she sprang from the bed and followed, passing him about halfway down. In the kitchen his dad was putting a tin of sardines on the floor by the waste bin. She went straight to them.

'They'll make your coat shine, Ka.'

'It shines already.'

But his dad was pulling on his coat and muttering about the Northern line. If he was going to try and get home a bit earlier he needed to set off now, he said.

'Now don't forget to lock up. You can leave the cat in. I've done her a litter tray of sorts. We can get her some of the proper stuff at the weekend. You can get her some Whiskas though.'

There was a box of soil by the back door and a pound coin on the table. The front door slammed shut.

'What do you think of sardines then?'

It was obvious she liked them.

'I know you can speak.'

She rubbed her mouth against his trouser leg, streaking it with oil. And she started to purr.

'*Who* are you, Ka? *What* are you?'

He wanted to know everything about her. And he wanted her to speak.

'Ka. Look at me.'

She started to wash herself, sitting on the floor with one leg in the air, paying particular attention to her white belly. The pads of her paws were like well polished leather, black and shiny, not worn at all. She was behaving like an ordinary cat.

'Ka. Answer me.' She carried on washing.

He went upstairs to clean his teeth, glanced in his room. The stone cat wasn't there. Of course not. And downstairs Ka was yowling. He ran down again. She was scratching at the back door.

'There's a litter tray, Ka.' He showed her.

And she looked disdainful. She gave him a cat sneer. Do you think I'm going to use that? In front of you? You must be mad.

So he let her out, watched her spring onto the fence and drop into Mrs Ewing's garden. Then he ran upstairs and watched from his bedroom window, saw her digging in Mr Ewing's newly dug seed bed, then squatting over the hole, her too-long tail upright and trembling. He couldn't help laughing.

And when he went to school he left her outside because she made it clear that was what she wanted. She was a cat, an ordinary cat with a mind of her own, and an extraordinary cat at the same time. He thought about her all day, but couldn't bring himself to buy cat food on the way home. To find her waiting for him was too much to hope.

But she was there on the back window-sill! As soon as he got inside the house he heard Number 33's dog barking, and rushed through to the kitchen. And there was a rigid Ka. Fortunately the dog, a terrier that hated cats, hated squirrels even more. It was hurling itself at the back fence where two of them were racing up and down, jeering. When Topher opened the door Ka shot inside, and Mrs Ewing appeared on the other side of the fence. She wore spiky curlers and looked like a hedgehog.

'New cat, Topher? Nice that. Snuffle snuffle.' She sounded like a hedgehog too. 'Shouldn't let her do that mind.' She poked her snout towards the kitchen. Ka was on the table.

'Your dad keeps it nice he does. Snuffle snuffle. Not many men like that I can tell you.'

Topher closed the door.

He put a saucer of milk on the floor. Ka sprang down and drank it quickly. 'Mwow!' It was obvious she was still hungry.

'All right. If you're staying.'

He ran to Angelo's, all the way there and halfway back, and he met Lisa.

'Got a cat, Topher?' She'd spotted the Salmon Supreme.

'No, a boa constrictor.'

She giggled. 'Can I come and see it? What's it like, Topher?'

'You wouldn't believe me if I told you.'

'Why not?'

She skipped along beside him, blonde bunches bouncing, a shiny new watch on her wrist. She always had some new toy or other. Her dad earned loads. He was a film director or something like that.

'I wouldn't stay long, Topher. I'm a bit jet-lagged actually. We've been on location in Spain, you know.'

Jet-lagged! From Spain! What a show off!

'I thought you had to enter another time zone for that.'

'What do you mean?'

There were a lot of show-offs in Arburton Road. They had posh cars and burglar alarms – which kept going off when there weren't any burglars.

'Can I come in then?' They were at his house. 'I like your door, Topher.'

'S'pose so.'

His dad said they were lucky to have such a nice house. They couldn't afford to buy it now. It had been his gran's. She and Mrs Ewing had been lifelong enemies, always complaining about each other's noise. He could hear Mrs Ewing's radio now, announcing a bomb scare at Paddington Station.

'Oooh, Topher, you are lucky. She's lovely.'

Ka was sitting at the end of the hall, on a black tile. She was very still and for a second he thought she'd turned to stone again. Then her tail twitched.

'What's her name?'

'Ka.'

'Car? That's a stupid name for a cat. Has she got wheels?'

'Ka. K.A.' He spelt it out. 'It's Egyptian . . .' For a double, he was going to say, but stopped himself. It was too complicated.

Ka followed them into the kitchen.

How could he explain, anyway? He didn't understand it himself. Now Ka was rolling over his feet, nearly standing on her head. I adore you. I adore you, she seemed to say. Seemed.

He laughed. 'You don't. You're just hungry.'

He opened the tin, and filled her dish. She purred ecstatically.

Lisa got down on her knees to watch. 'Where did you

get her?'

'She just turned up.'

'Perhaps she came from a different time zone.'

He thought she was just using the words, trying to prove she had understood about jet-lag and time zones, but she obviously meant something different.

'Dad made this film once. About a cat. It could travel through time. Cats can, Jodie says.'

Jodie was Lisa's big sister. She was into astrology and nail varnish, a different colour on every nail.

Topher laughed. 'Jodie's crazy.'

But it was odd how what she'd said fitted into his thoughts.

Soon after that his dad came in and Lisa went home.

Thursday – liver. His dad got two pieces from the freezer and put them in the microwave.

'Chips or rice?'

'Chips.'

While they were cooking he went up to change and came down smelling of aftershave.

'How do I look?'

'Fine.'

'You don't mind me going out, do you, Topher?'

''Course not.'

'I wish you would go out more.'

'I don't like going out.'

They ate their meal in silence and his dad went out soon afterwards.

Actually he didn't like staying in either, not on his own. But it was better with Ka, not so lonely. The house seemed warmer, somehow. She slept on his knee – till a football match came on the telly. Then she watched it, her eyes following the ball, and as the game speeded up so did she. She got off his knee and started to pat the ball with her paw, standing on her hind legs as she got more and more excited. And she won! Or looked as if she had when she eventually climbed back onto his knee. Then she fell asleep purring loudly.

He should have gone to bed straight after the match, but he hadn't got the heart to disturb her. Or was it simply that he didn't want to go up to his bedroom? That he didn't want the night to come? It was cosy here with the gas fire flickering and popping. And Ka was real and she seemed to have been here for ever. She was a warm breathing cat, a playful purring cat. She had been stone. Now she was fur.

But what might happen in the middle of the night?

Chapter 6

So that's how his dad found them, asleep in the chair. He hustled Topher to bed and put Ka outside, but even before he'd got his pyjamas on Topher heard her at the window. He let her in. She sprang onto the bed. When he got in she pushed her way under the duvet. His dad heard her purring when he came in to say goodnight.

'Oh there she is.' He lifted the cover slightly. 'A sort of furry hot water bottle. 'Night, Topher.'

'Goodnight, Dad. Goodnight, Ka.' Topher stroked between her ears, encouraging her to stay where he could feel her. And she 'owned' him, pressing her cheek against his several times. He had to laugh – she did the same against the fridge! Still fearful though, he tried hard to stay awake, but his eyes kept closing, and after a bit, feeling her padding to her usual place at the bottom of the bed, he fell asleep. And that was where he found her in the morning!

And so it went on. When he went to school, he put her outside, because she was a free spirit; there was no point in keeping her prisoner. When he returned she was waiting on the doorstep, or sometimes further up the street, in the tree outside Number 58, making the dog there go batty. Then she would spring down and race Topher to Number 35, not that Topher was racing, but she pretended that he was, smirking with success as she sat by the milk waiting for him. When he remembered, Topher tried not to get too fond of her, but if he tried to keep his distance the closer she tried to get. She would push her way under the bedclothes or sit on a book he was trying to read. If he went to bed early while she was still outside, she would wake him by scratching on the window, sometimes in the middle of the night. When Topher started to look bleary-eyed at breakfast his dad fixed a cat-flap in the back door.

'It's best if we encourage her to use the back way. Safer that way. We don't want her out the front on the road.'

Ka rewarded his kindness by refusing to sit on his knee, even when he enticed her with small pieces of cheese which she loved. She preferred Topher's knee, Topher's feet, Topher's anything.

'She likes you, Topher,' his dad said one evening.

'Go away, Ka.'

Mr Hope was reading a book by the fire. They had put it on because it was quite chilly, despite being June. Topher was trying to play a computer game called 'Secret of the Tomb' and the cat was delicately – it seemed deliberately – stepping on the keys.

His dad laughed.

Topher was a bit annoyed. He was at an interesting point. Zastaph, slave to Artan, was asking the Moon Goddess:

Where hast thou come from, O mistress?

and Ka's paws had produced a lot of nonsense. It looked like algebra, letters and numbers mixed together.

He was about to delete them, when his dad looked up, said, 'Hold on a sec. Do you see what she's written? What a coincidence. Bubastis, that's in Egypt or was in ancient times.'

He got up and stroked the cat's head. 'You're a clever cat, Ka. Come from Egypt, have you? Like the cat Tessa brought back.'

Tessa was his mum's name. Topher hated his dad saying it, but he didn't know why. Part of him wanted to talk about his mum.

His dad stroked the cat. 'She would have liked you, Ka. She really would.'

'She's a nuisance, a so-and-so nuisance.' Topher tipped her on the floor, but didn't delete what she had written. It was of course a coincidence, odd nevertheless. And Ka was staring at him. No she wasn't, she was staring past him. It was her superior look. It said, You are being very stupid, Topher.

Several thoughts went through his mind. He pushed back the ones about his mum, and the ones about Ka's double life, then changed his mind. Perhaps he could say something?

'Dad . . .'

But now his dad wasn't listening. He was staring into the fire. What was he thinking about? He looked sad. Still, a bit of Topher wanted to say something. Why was it so difficult? He went to get a drink.

When he came back the computer was switched off.

'Sorry. I thought you'd gone to bed, son.'

Topher switched it back on and, as quickly as he could,

he played the game up to the point he had reached before, but Ka's writing wasn't there.

'Where is Ka?' He thought he could hear her purring.

'Look.' Mr Hope lifted his book. She was on his knee.

'Traitor.'

But he couldn't be cross with Ka for long.

Coming home to Ka was better than coming home to an empty house. Coming home to Ka when you were down in the dumps because some stupid teacher had told you off for something you hadn't done was definitely better. And that was what happened next day.

'I'm surprised at you, Topher,' Miss Crabb had said, 'I'll see you later.'

Worse, she hadn't seen him later, hadn't given him the chance to explain. She'd thought he was being rude to Ellie, the new girl, the deaf girl, when in fact he'd been trying to say something to her. He'd tried out some sign language, finger spelling, which he'd learned from his free leaflet. The new girl had just answered a question in class. She had shouted. In fact it sounded as if she was chewing and shouting at the same time and Titch Warren had sniggered, tapping the side of his head as if to say, 'She's barmy.' Miss Crabb hadn't seen him, but the new girl had. That's when Topher had started to spell out YOU'RE OK. HE'S AN IDIOT, but Miss Crabb obviously thought he was making a rude sign. What a mess.

He switched on the television. It was a quiz show.

'It's not fair, Ka.'

She sympathised, rubbing her cheeks against his. Then she settled on his knee. Purred.

Don't worr..rr..y. Don't worr..rrr..y, she seemed to

say. Seemed, he was quite sure about that. Now and again he thought about the night she had spoken to him but not often because he couldn't bear the thought of her being stone. What if she turned back?

Don't worr..rry. Don't worr..rry.

She stretched full length so that her body trembled and her paws straddled his neck, and there she stayed, her head under his chin, purring. Throbbing.

Don't worr..rr..y. Don't worr..rr..y. Don't worr..rr..y.

He changed channels with the remote control but disturbed her when he laughed at an elephant on stilts, and she hissed, pressed a claw into his shoulder.

'Don't do that, fish-breath.'

She tucked her paws beneath her, started to purr again. Sorr..rr..y. Sorr..rr..y. She was comforting and comfortable again. Then the doorbell rang. He let it ring, didn't want to get up. But whoever it was was insistent. Persistent, they must have their finger on the bell. So he got up, putting Ka on the warm patch where he had been sitting, before he opened the door.

At first he didn't realise who it was. She looked different out of school, in jeans and a Save the Whale sweatshirt and her dark hair was loose. And she just stood in the doorway saying nothing, going red, clutching a couple of Mars bars.

'I j-just . . .'

'Hello . . .' They spoke together. Laughed.

'You first,' said Topher. He didn't know what to say anyway.

Ellie Wentworth's voice was a whisper this time. It was hard to hear what she was saying.

'I just . . .' Then she thrust a note and two Mars bars into his hands. The note said, 'I just wanted to say that I knew what you wanted to say and thanks.' Then she turned to go, but stopped as Ka came into the hall.

'Nice cat.'

'Stroke her.' He made sure Ellie could see his face. That's what the leaflet had said you should do. Some deaf people lipread. He hoped Ka would let Ellie stroke her. It didn't look as if she was going to. She'd looked and gone back to the sitting room.

'Come in.' Topher closed the front door. 'Come and see her.'

Ka was on the settee washing herself. Ellie knelt in front of her. Topher offered her one of the Mars bars. She waved it away.

'No yours.'

'No yours.' He insisted.

'Thank you.'

'No thank *you*.'

It was awkward. There was no doubt about that. The leaflet had said, 'Speak in short sentences – each with a single thought.' It had also said, 'Deaf doesn't mean dim.' Ellie wasn't dim. She wouldn't be in his maths group if she were, but he sounded as if he thought she was. He knew he did.

She was stroking Ka's neck now, and Ka was purring, head back, eyes closed. Could Ellie hear her purr? She turned to Topher and signalled that he should put his hand where she'd had hers and when he did he felt Ka's throat vibrating.

In class Ellie had worn a hearing device round her neck, and so had the teacher. She was wearing it now.

Topher pointed to it, and then to his own chest. She delved into the bag she was carrying and brought out the thing the teacher had worn. With it round his neck things were better. He could talk more normally, though he still had the problem of what to say.

Fortunately Ka decided to be entertaining. A fly had appeared from somewhere, and started buzzing round the room. First she watched, wriggling her bottom and twitching her tail. Then she leaped onto it but missed, then she chased it from one side of the room to the other just missing ornaments and pictures – till at last she caught and ate it.

'YUK!' Ellie and Topher laughed together. And the doorbell rang again. It was Lisa with a squeaky mouse for Ka.

His dad was really pleased when he came home and found them all there. He went out to Angelo's and bought Coke and crisps for everyone; he said Ellie and Lisa must come round as often as they liked. Topher could read his thoughts. Topher was coping. Topher was getting back to normal – and Topher thought perhaps he was.

Then Ka disappeared.

Chapter 7

It was a Thursday. He came home from school and she wasn't there. She wasn't in the street, and she wasn't on the front doorstep. She wasn't in the hall or the kitchen. The house felt cold and grey. He started to feel scared as he climbed the stairs, hardly dared to enter his bedroom. What if the stone cat was on the cupboard beside his bed? It wasn't, but he found it a few minutes later, under the bed, thick with dust, as if it had been there for a long time. As if it had been knocked off the cupboard and pushed under the bed with the usual clobber that gets lost under beds, socks, comics and shoes. He didn't know what to think. She wasn't in the garden or in the shed.

'I don't care.' He closed the shed door and Mrs Ewing poked her spiky head through the hedge.

'Looking for your pussycat, are you? Don't worry, she'll be back. Cats wander you know.'

Ellie came round. She took Ka's dish into the back garden and banged it with a spoon, and all the time she called Ka's name. Mrs Ewing complained about the noise but Ellie didn't hear her. She did stop, but only while she went to the front door, where she started to bang an empty milk bottle and call again. Lisa arrived, but went out immediately to search the nearby streets. When she came back she said she hadn't found her alive, but neither had she found her squished. She had found a squished one in Fitzwarren Gardens. It was horrible, she said.

'I don't care.'

Lisa gasped. Ellie told her that Topher didn't mean it. Soon after that Lisa went home. Ellie made some tea. Then she went home. It was her piano lesson tonight. Topher wasn't surprised about that any more, now that she'd explained how she felt the sounds vibrating, just as she felt Ka's purring. Ka's purring. It hurt to think about it. His dad tried to cheer him up. Everybody tried to cheer him up.

'Ah, Topher. Don't be upset. She'll be back.'

'I'm not upset.'

'Cats wander you know.'

It was Thursday: liver and bacon – Ka's favourite, but she wasn't there to eat the leftovers, which was most of Topher's helping because he didn't like it much. She wasn't there at bedtime.

He dusted the stone cat and placed it carefully on the middle of his bedside cupboard, so that it couldn't fall off. Then he picked it up again, breathed on it, rubbed it on his pyjamas. But still it looked dull, alike yet unlike Ka. It looked lifeless, even with the lamplight shining on it. It was lifeless. As he put the lamp out, he willed the statue to come back to life, to wake him in the night, but it didn't even glow as it had before. Nothing woke him in the middle of the night and Ka wasn't there in the morning.

He kept a lookout for her on the way to school – and for 'squished' ones – though he hardly dare look at these. All the roads round Archway roared with traffic.

When he got to school Ellie came rushing up.

'Has Ka . . . ?'

'No.'

They searched the school grounds. At lunchtime they asked permission to leave the premises and search outside. Miss Crabb said no. She didn't think it was a good idea, not without their parents' permission. She also said, 'Don't worry, Topher. She'll be back. Cats wander you know.'

Topher felt like strangling her.

Ka wasn't there when he got home.

She stayed away all weekend.

She didn't come back on Monday and Tuesday.

Lisa said that Jodie said Ka was almost certainly timetravelling. Topher told Lisa to tell Jodie to get lost. He began to hate everybody. Above all he hated the stone cat beside his bed.

Then Ka was back! After a whole week away. He found her on his bed one Friday when he went to change out of his uniform.

'Ka!'

She hardly stirred. He lay beside her, buried his face in her fur, loving its musky smell. She was in a deep sleep.

'Where have you been, Ka? Have you been far?' He lifted a hind paw. The pads were black and shiny, not worn at all. So she hadn't been far.

'Have you been hiding, Ka? Where? Why?'

She was very tired. He stayed with her, curled round her. He couldn't leave, couldn't disturb her to take her downstairs.

And that was how his dad found them when he came

home, both fast asleep on the bed. Topher woke to the friendly smell of fish and chips and his dad's hand ruffling his hair. Fish and chips, from the shop; it must be Friday. Great! Everything was great!

'What are you so happy about, son?'

'Look!' Topher moved aside.

Usually on Fridays, Ka met Mr Hope at the door. She would jump on the hallstand and try to nudge open the newspaper with her nose. Today it was a full minute before the smell of fish reached her. When it did they saw her nose twitch first. Then she looked up, yawned and stretched, and all the time her movements were getting faster and faster. Her pink nose was whiffling. Then she sprang from the bed and followed them downstairs, her tail quivering.

'Mwa! Mwa!'

'Where did you go, Ka?'

It was after dinner and Topher was half-heartedly playing on his computer. Ka was on his knee watching the cursor, occasionally batting it with her paw. His dad was reading the paper.

'I reckon she's found an old lady who'll feed her fresh salmon,' his dad said.

'You don't like fresh salmon do you, Ka? Tell me, where do you go?'

And then something extraordinary happened. Ka stepped onto the keyboard – as she had done a few weeks ago – and carefully spelled out:

$$*B-+uBasT*is$$

Again!

'Look at this, Dad.'

Mr Hope glanced over his shoulder. 'Blimey. Ha.'

'Ka did it.'

'Ha. Clever cat. Or clever Topher.'

'It wasn't me, Dad.'

But Mr Hope went back to his paper. He obviously thought Topher was joking. And Topher didn't bother to explain, though he needed to talk about it to someone. Something very strange was happening. It would be good if he had some evidence. Carefully he pressed EXIT and SAVE.

Chapter 8

Bubastis. His dad had said it was in Egypt, Ancient Egypt. Ka had written it twice. Had she been to Bubastis? How? Topher turned to ask her, wondering if she would speak as well as write, but she was at the door, scratching, making it very clear that she wanted to go outside. He opened the door and let her into the kitchen where the cat-flap was. Then he went upstairs.

Bubastis. He searched for it in one of his books about Egypt. He had lots now because he'd brought his mother's books up to his room. This one was about architecture. Bubastis wasn't in the index, but he leafed through it anyway. It had lots of pictures mostly of magnificent palaces. They had vast halls with massive square entrances – no archways because the Egyptians didn't know how to make those – and wide courtyards with richly painted columns. And in the large rooms were small ones, inner sanctuaries, where statues of the gods were kept. Gods! He still found this hard to take in. They looked more like birds and animals; they had the heads of birds and animals, but they were worshipped as gods because they were believed to be their *kas* – or doubles!

Now his heartbeat quickened, for there in front of him was a beautiful cat in a shrine lined with gold, and the caption beneath said it was the goddess Bastet in

Bubastis. Made of bronze, she also took the form of a living cat it said. In Ancient Egypt people depended on cats, and they worshipped them. What? All of them? This doubles business was complicated. He read on. Real cats were prized because they protected the corn supplies from rats and mice, and because *any one of them* might be the goddess. And it was in Bubastis that the festival of Bastet was celebrated. He read it several times to be sure. 'The worshippers travelled in barges along a tributary of the Nile to Bubastis . . . On reaching Bubastis they celebrated the festival with vast quantities of wine and elaborate sacrifices.'

His thoughts raced ahead. Bubastis. Was that where Ka went? That's what she'd written. Was she a time-travelling cat? It wasn't just time she would have to travel through; Egypt was thousands of miles away. Was it possible? Topher wished she would come in, wished she would speak to him, wished that he was cleverer. Maybe then he would understand. A time-travelling cat? It was a crazy idea though perhaps not, if what Old Charlie had said about time was true.

Outside, rain dribbled down the glass, blurring the lights of London, soft-edging the buildings. Where was Ka now? Had she gone again? Would she return? It was getting darker. A star appeared. He opened the window and called her. She hated the rain. Surely she would come in? She didn't so he got ready for bed, closed the window because the rain was wetting the curtains.

And she appeared a little later – scrabble-scratching against the glass, streaking it with mud.

'You're double trouble, Ka.' He raised the sash and she came in, like a limbo dancer! Then she purred loudly

41

while rubbing herself against him, drying her fur on his pyjama legs. He got back into bed and she licked his feet, her rough tongue tickling between his toes. Later she washed herself, licking the inside of her left foreleg, rubbing her face against the wet fur.

'Don't forget behind your ears, Ka.'

She hadn't forgotten; she was using her paw like a flannel, drawing it elegantly over her head, pulling the ear forward, letting it flick back.

'What's Bubastis like, Ka?'

She had finished washing, but ignored the question. She was circling now, lightly marking the bottom sheet with muddy paw prints.

'Are you flattening the reeds, Ka? That's what Egyptian cats did before they slept by the river.'

But she didn't answer, for she was already asleep, her warm fur against his feet.

It took Topher longer to settle. There were too many thoughts in his head. But when he did sleep nothing woke him in the night.

The following day, a Saturday, he went round to see Ellie. He left Ka asleep on his bed. He needed to talk about what had happened. It was difficult talking to Ellie, there was no doubt about that, but when you did make yourself clear, she was very understanding. You had to say things in a straightforward way. Ellie was straightforward too. Soon after they'd met she'd asked, 'Where's your mother?' and he'd said, 'She's dead.' And that was that. They knew where they stood. Then she'd told him about getting ill and becoming deaf when she was eight. He'd said, 'That was bad,' and she'd said, 'Not as bad as your mum dying.'

He liked the way she'd said dying, not like most people, who if they mentioned it at all, talked about 'losing your mother' – as if he'd left her lying around somewhere.

Ellie lived in Cheverton Road, two streets away. The Wentworths were noisy and untidy and lots of fun. They all joined in to give Ellie as much talking practice as they could, even her younger brothers, Russell and Luke. She needed lots of practice because when you can't hear people talking, and you can't hear yourself, you don't know if you're pronouncing words properly. That's why her voice sounded wonky.

When Topher arrived she was reading *Dick Whittington* to Russell – Russell the Brussel – who had just collapsed in giggles. He was rolling about the floor. Ellie was laughing too. It seemed she'd just said, 'Dick Whittington's cat went on a chip' instead of 'on a ship'. 'Sh' and 'ch' were two sounds she often muddled. Topher wanted to speak to her alone, but he had to wait till she'd finished the story. Then Russell wanted them both to play with him, so they went to Waterlow Park to get some peace.

But Ellie wasn't her usual attentive self. They sat on a bench facing one another so that she could lipread, but she kept looking at a grey squirrel in a waste paper basket. She asked him to tell her again. He felt stupid repeating it all; he thought that someone would overhear and think he was crazy, till he realised that no one was taking any notice. The bag lady on the bench opposite was busy feeding the pigeons. You could hardly see her, there were so many, and the man next to her on the grass was slowly rotating while standing on his head.

Maybe the whole world was crazy! So he tried again, and this time she thought he was joking.

'I'm not joking!' He couldn't help shouting, and the grey squirrel shot up a tree.

'Show me then!' She shouted so loudly that all the pigeons flew off the bag lady.

So they set off for Topher's house, walking over Archway Bridge and down Fitzwarren Gardens – and he thought about Dick Whittington and his cat. Why hadn't he thought of it before? This was Dick Whittington territory. Fitzwarren was the name of the merchant whose ship had taken Dick's cat to the east. The Whittington Hospital was in Archway Road, below the bridge. Wasn't there a commemorative plaque somewhere? He thought of asking Ellie, but decided it would only complicate matters, and matters were complicated enough. They walked in silence. But maybe there had always been magical cats in these parts. Could Dick's cat talk and write? He thought she'd made his fortune, just by being a good mouser.

There was a mouse, a headless one, on the doorstep when they reached home, but Ka wasn't around. He led Ellie into the sitting room, switched on the computer and opened the game he'd been playing. And there, to his great relief, was the word.

*B−+uBasT*is

They both stared at it, then he touched Ellie's arm so that she would look at him. 'I asked her where she had been, and she wrote that.' Ellie listened like an alert dog, her head slightly to one side.

'Yes. You said.'

'Twice. She wrote it twice.'

'Yes.'

'But do you believe me?'

It was very important that she said yes.

'Bubastis. That's in Ancient Egypt, isn't it?' She'd seen a programme about it on the telly.

He noticed she didn't say yes.

But she had seen the word in the British Museum. She'd been lots of times, she said – to the British Museum, not Bubastis. The Egyptian rooms were really interesting. There were lots of cats there, statues of cats and dead ones, made into mummies.

He'd been – with his mother. It was creepy.

He tried to explain. 'Bubastis was where they had a cat festival. To celebrate the goddess Bastet. She was a cat goddess.'

Ellie knew – that's what the programme had been about. 'But Ka couldn't have gone to Egypt, Topher. It's too far.'

Her face was always very expressive. It was obvious she thought he was barmy. 'She might have gone to the British Museum, but why?' Now she looked baffled.

'Ellie . . .' He wanted to say that if Ka could leave messages on a computer she could do anything, but before he could get the words out his dad came in and started talking about school.

And by the end of the weekend he thought he might as well go to the British Museum. He might find a clue there. After all he couldn't go to Ancient Egypt in search of Ka, and by Sunday night she still hadn't returned. He'd searched the neighbourhood several times, spent hours calling and tapping her dish, but she'd

45

stayed away.

When he went to bed the stone cat seemed brighter and when he put out the light it glowed. His hopes rose, but in the morning it was still beside his bed and there was no purring Ka at his feet. Stone stayed stone.

Chapter 9

At breakfast his dad was cheerful.

'I think we should get Ka a name tag, with her address on it. It's obvious she's got a second home somewhere – cats often do that – but if the other person knew they'd return her to us, or at least stop feeding her.'

'I want to go and look for her.'

'You can't. It's school.'

'Ellie said she thought she might be in the British Museum.'

His dad wasn't listening.

'I'll buy a tag and get it engraved on the way home. It'll be ready when she returns.' He was picking up his briefcase. 'Don't worry, Topher. She will come back.'

The door slammed and the house felt cold and empty, as if everything in it was made of stone.

Topher wanted Ka badly. Now. He couldn't possibly concentrate on lessons so he waited a bit so as not to bump into anyone on their way to school, then he set off. The British Museum must be worth a try.

It wasn't. He found cats all right, hundreds of them, but none of them was real, and he made an idiot of himself talking to one of them right at the start. It was in a glass case in a darkened gallery. Spotlit, it stood in a pool of light and it was beautiful. Sacred to Bastet, the label said.

'Ka?'

He didn't realise he'd spoken till he felt a girl looking at him, then he moved away sharpish and didn't come back till he'd seen her leave the gallery. In the meantime he'd had some thoughts and looked at a lot more cats. The one in the case was made of bronze. It had a gold ring through its nose and the eye of Horus round its neck. It looked like one he'd seen in a book but it didn't look like Ka. None of the cats did. There were about twenty in the case in front of him, most of them tiny. One was part of a ring. None of them had Ka's beautiful markings, yet they were all kas, a notice said, and all sacred to Bastet.

As always the doubles thing confused him utterly. He went and sat down on a leather bench and tried to decide exactly what he was looking for. Was it the live Ka or her double? He didn't know, that was the trouble. There certainly weren't any live cats here; he was wasting his time. He should never have bunked off school.

'What d'y make of that then?' An American woman was sitting herself beside him. She had earrings like parrots and at first he thought she was talking to him. Then he noticed a boy the other side of her. They were both looking at a fat baboon.

'Great, Mom, it looks just like Pop.'

They laughed, punched one another in a friendly fight. Topher got up and walked away.

Shortly afterwards he found himself looking at a huge stone falcon and its painted eye was staring at him; it was black and white and really seemed to be staring. In fact eyes seemed to be watching him from all over – including those of the attendant. She looked really sus-

48

picious as if she was going to pounce at any moment. What are you doing all alone, boy? Why aren't you at school and what have you done with your mother? He really ought to be going; he must make sure he got home before his father. That was daft. It was still morning, wasn't it? Perhaps he should go to afternoon school?

He left the gallery, left the museum soon afterwards, after a swift tour upstairs. The galleries were full of Egyptian stuff – coffins and mummies of all sorts of things. Spooky. He didn't see Bubastis mentioned anywhere – so much for Ellie's memory – but when he walked out of the underground at Archway, there was a hoarding with Horus the falcon on it. It was an advert for Egypt Airways. The plane was called Horus and there was a picture of the falcon on its side. Fly into the past, it urged. He wished he could. If only . . . He tried to cheer himself up. If only, if only Ka was waiting for him at home.

She wasn't but his father was.

Topher was in deep trouble.

Chapter 10

'Where have you been?'

His dad was angry. Topher had never seen him so angry. Miss Crabb had rung him at work. She'd tried home first. Was Topher ill? she'd said. How long was he going to be ill? They needed him for the special school assembly the next day.

'I felt a fool. I said you were fine and that you were at school. She said you weren't. I was worried sick.'

He'd rung home and got no reply. Then he'd left work straightaway – broken his precious routine – come home, found the place empty, rang the police.

'I thought you might have been . . .'

He didn't finish, but went to the phone. Topher heard him telling someone that his son was home now, that everything was all right. Was it? When he returned he looked as if he was trying to swallow something disgusting.

'That was the police. They said I shouldn't have panicked. Lots of boys your age sag off from school.'

Sag?

'Play truant! Say they're going to school and then go off and do something else. Stealing usually.'

'You don't think . . .'

'I don't know what to think. I thought I could trust you, Topher.'

'I went to the British Museum.'

'Why?'

'To look for Ka.'

'You're crazy.' There didn't seem any point trying to explain. His dad hummed and hawed about whether to take him back to school, decided it was too late, said he ought to go back to work anyway and left, slamming the door. It was about half past two.

Topher went down the garden to the garden shed where he had first found Ka. The newspapers on which she'd been sleeping had gone. More recent ones were stacked tidily at one side. Was it really nearly two months ago? He went out and searched the street again. Council workers were re-surfacing the footpath opposite, pouring thick black tar over the old path where small yellow flowers had pushed their way through the tarmac. The road roller was standing by to flatten the new tar, and the flowers underneath. It seemed typical somehow.

Then Ellie appeared – at a run and arms waving. Her voice when she started to speak was all over the place. She didn't notice how fed up he was. They went inside. She thrust a leaflet into his hand. She'd been to the hospital and she could have it, she said.

'It.' She pointed to the leaflet. It was about an operation on the ear, a cochlear implant. She read over his shoulder, pointing to bits she thought he should read. If it worked the operation would help a lot. It would help her hear some sounds, her own voice for instance, so she would know how loud or soft it was and be able to control it more.

She was very excited.

51

'That would be great, Ellie.'

Actually the leaflet made him feel sick. All that stuff about cutting the head open and putting electrodes inside. Wasn't it dangerous? She seemed to read his mind. 'It's worth a try, Topher.'

'Go for it, Ellie.' He sounded false – and her face was sort of flickering as it did when she was trying to put something difficult into words. Then she blurted it out, a series of blurts really.

'Look, Topher. There are some things . . . you can't change. You know that. I know that. And if . . .'

He finished her sentence for her, which usually made her mad.

'If you can't change them you have to accept them.'

'But if you can change them, you've got to try, haven't you?'

They could do the operation quite soon she said. 'You'll come and see me in hospital, won't you?'

'Sure.'

He hated hospitals – and he liked her the way she was.

She touched his hand. 'I'll need your help.'

He made them both a cup of tea.

Later she asked about Ka, and he told her she still hadn't returned.

'But she will, Topher.'

He didn't say anything and she looked annoyed and said, 'For someone called Hope you haven't got much, have you?'

But she stayed till his dad came home.

He was still in a bad mood and went on and on about Topher's crimes while he cooked the dinner – Monday,

Shepherd's pie. But then suddenly, as he put the plates on the table, he said, 'Anyway that's behind us now, though you'll have to face the music at school tomorrow. But as long as you never do anything like that again we'll forget it. Right?'

Topher said okay. Later, he asked his dad if he would write to school and explain that he'd been worried about Ka and had gone to look for her. His dad said no, that it had been a stupid thing to do, and that if he wrote a letter like that it would look as if he were condoning it, and he didn't.

Topher went to bed early and longed for Ka's return. His mum would have written a letter. He knew she would.

Chapter 11

Ka didn't return.

At school next day Miss Crabb said, 'What got into you, Topher? Do you want to tell me all about it?' And he thought he might, but when he mentioned Ka she said, 'Oh that cat again. I'm not sure she's worth all the trouble she puts you to. Cats don't care, Topher. Tell your dad to get you a dog.'

He didn't want a dog. He wanted Ka – whether she cared or not. But she stayed away. His dad was away a lot too, he seemed to work longer hours and go out more at nights. Sylvia from the office was mentioned quite a lot. His dad brought her home once, for a meal before they went out to play tennis. She was freckly with reddish-brown hair, and she laughed a lot showing big horse teeth. She brought Topher a computer game. His dad said she was a whiz on computers. She got on Topher's nerves. They both did.

It was July now, summer, but it didn't feel summery. Arburton Road was leafy, and noisy with children playing and the ice-cream van fanfaring and dogs barking at cats. They sat just out of reach on walls and window-sills, but Ka wasn't among them. Topher gave up looking for her as he trudged home from school, gave up expecting to see her on the porch or curled up on his duvet, gave up expecting the little stone cat to be anything other than stone. He put it back in the cupboard. Ka had gone and that was that.

Then Ellie went too. One Thursday she wasn't in school. That evening her mum rang to say she had been called in to hospital suddenly. There had been a cancellation and she was next on the list for the operation.

'She would love to see you, Topher. Can we give you a lift sometime?'

'Er.'

'Well, give us a ring when you want to. You've got our number, haven't you?'

She rang off.

Now he loathed himself. Ellie wanted him but he hadn't the guts to go and see her.

Next day during PE in the schoolyard he thought he saw Ka. She was in the garden of the house opposite the school. It was near the end of the lesson, and when everyone else went in, he hung back then shot over the road. The cat wasn't there; nor was she next door. He went and searched the back gardens and thought he saw her again disappearing into a garden further up.

'Ka!' He climbed onto the fence, and a hand grabbed his ankle.

'Ah, it's you, is it? You're the one who's had my owls, are you?' The man looked a bit like an owl himself, bald with thick glasses. 'Where are they then?'

He pulled Topher off the fence.

'I d-don't know what you mean.'

'Come on, tell me where they are and I'll let you off.' The man had hold of his collar now.

'I don't know what you mean!'

'Right, we're going over the road.' The man jerked

his head towards the school. 'You ought to be in there, I bet.'

Things were going from bad to worse. Minutes later they were standing in front of the Headmaster, Mr Westlake. It seemed the owls were two concrete ones which used to stand on the gateposts of the man's house. They had disappeared two nights ago.

'I was at home two nights ago.'

'How do I know that?' The man was called Mr Cleveland.

'You can ask my dad.'

Mr Westlake was already picking up the phone.

'Good thinking, Topher. Get me Mr Hope's work number will you please, Valerie.' He was speaking to the school secretary, but he turned to Mr Cleveland. 'I think you can leave this in our hands, now.'

Mr Cleveland looked as if he was made of concrete. 'Really, Mr Cleveland. I will be in touch with you.'

Reluctantly the owl-owner left the room and Topher thought he'd go back to the classroom, but the Head had other ideas.

'Just a minute, Topher. Sit down, lad. We still have a few things to talk about, what you were doing over the road for a start. Isn't this the second time you've been out of school during lesson time?'

Topher explained.

Mr Westlake looked grave. He looked even graver a few moments later after he'd answered the phone.

'Your father says he can't be sure where you were the night before last. He was out most of the evening.'

Topher didn't know why he bothered going home that afternoon, to a father who didn't trust him, who didn't stick up for him. Not that he was home when Topher let himself in, but he soon would be, and then there would be more trouble.

When the doorbell rang he hoped it was Ellie, then remembered where she was, and felt worse. It was Lisa. She was off to Spain with her mum and dad, she said. Her dad was making a film, a Western, a funny one. She started to tell him the plot but it didn't seem very funny. He just wondered what it must be like to be going to Spain with your mum and dad.

'What about school?'

'My mum will give me lessons, me and Michael.' Michael was her little brother. 'Jodie's staying with a friend.'

Lucky old Lisa.

When his dad came home, he put fish and chips on the table. Then he got plates, and didn't say anything. It was worse than shouting. Topher couldn't eat anything. His dad put the unopened packet in the bin. Then he went into his study and disappeared behind a book. It was called *A Brief History of Time*. Later, Topher took him a cup of tea, thought he would try to talk to him.

'Aren't you going out tonight?' His dad usually went to the pub on Fridays.

'I can't, can I?'

'Why not?'

'Because I can't trust you.'

'Why not?'

But his dad didn't want to discuss anything, didn't want to hear his side of the story, didn't want to see him it seemed. He just carried on reading.

Topher went upstairs to his bedroom. For several minutes he stood at the window watching a hawk hovering in the sky several blocks away. At least he thought it was a hawk though it was unusual to see one in these parts. It hovered for quite a while, as if it were watching something below, but didn't swoop. When it flew away Topher opened a book, he thought he might do some homework, but he changed his mind. What was the point? He was in trouble at school. Nobody noticed when he did anything good, only when he was bad. Or they thought he was bad. He hadn't stolen those owls, but nobody believed him. They all thought he was a thief.

Suddenly he rushed downstairs, opened the study door and yelled, 'Who do you think I am? Why can't you help me?'

His dad didn't reply, didn't even look at him. And he hadn't drunk the tea Topher had made him. Feeling like an insect Topher crept back upstairs. Then he cried himself to sleep.

But he woke up in the night. Something was tapping on the window.

Chapter 12

It wasn't Ka. He'd shot to the window, thinking it was of course – there was something red and he thought it was her open mouth – but it wasn't.

Not Ka. Not Ka. That thought filled his mind as he pressed his face against the glass. Not Ka. Then tap-TAP! The glass vibrated against his nose and slowly, as he strained to see, the redness in front of him took shape. There were claws outside. Claws! Enormous red talons were gripping the windowledge on the other side of the glass, and red scaly legs stretched up from them into the darkness.

TAP! TAP! Whatever it was, was impatient now.

Topher looked up sharply, and deciphered the shape of an enormous bird.

A falcon – of course!

But how big! Bigger than an eagle, bigger than he was, much bigger than he was. It towered above him!

TAP! Its enormous beak crashed against the glass.

'Don't do that, you'll break it. I'll open it.' How odd. But, as he glanced down, to take hold of the window and push it up, something even odder dawned on him, for he saw his own feet on the window-sill. Then Topher realised that the bird outside only seemed enormous because he, Topher was tiny. How? When had it happened?

'Ker. Ker.' Or was it Ka. Ka?

Come out. Come out – it seemed to say. Open up.

Heaving up the window took all his strength and left him with hardly enough energy to climb through the gap he had made. But he did and found himself on the roof tiles, panting beneath the bird's hooked beak.

'Ker. Ker.' Again the beak opened and closed. Get on my back. Get on my back.

'How?' Topher shivered in his pyjamas as he peered up at the bird's grey breast.

'Ker. Ker.' The bird jerked its head.

'To the back.' Was that what it was saying? It seemed a better bet, so to the back he went, and there was the falcon's tail just touching his roof. Its stiff feathers separated beneath his hands and feet as he climbed, forming a springy ladder. Then there he was at the top, and up went the falcon's tail like a see-saw, tipping him into the hollow of the bird's back. And he landed on his bum!

Was this the hawk he had watched earlier, hovering over the Chersey Street flats? It reminded him of something.

'Ker!' With a cry the bird swivelled its head to reveal a black and white eye! Of course! Horus the falcon, that's who it was! Topher held on as the majestic bird strode forward, rocking him gently from side to side. He held on and all around him the lights of London glittered and flashed like a spectacular model of Legoland. Strings of lights marked roads and railway lines, shining squares the windows of houses and hotels. He held on tight, his arms round the bird's neck as it strode to the edge of the roof and stopped; and in the distance the dome of St. Paul's Cathedral shone softly and the Post Office tower winked. And even further away a red light sparked rhythmically – off on off on – never stopping. It was a pylon his dad had said, a radio aerial which picked up signals from all over the universe. The universe! He felt he was at its centre!

Beneath him the falcon stiffened and looking down Topher saw its red talons gripping the gutter, which was stuffed with old leaves. Further down he saw the garden path and the drain cover glimmering in the moonlight. He thought he saw a snail, then feeling dizzy he looked up again. Now inches from his own head the falcon's was turning slowly like a radar detector. From left to right, then right to left a hundred and eighty degrees each time, it was taking bearings. Then suddenly it stopped, seemed to have the information it needed. Then knowing where it was going, it stared straight ahead, and again Topher felt its body tense beneath him, and he tensed as he felt a rush of energy and a massive draught as the bird's wings rose and fell and rose again.

Then the roof was no longer beneath them, but miraculously they were not falling but flying, soaring up, up, up, into the night sky. Ghost-like the nightdress on Mrs Ewing's washing-line danced for a second then became a speck as buildings, trees, roads and the winding River Thames all shrank beneath him. Lights grew smaller then vanished leaving only darkness below and silence, for Horus the falcon was flying faster than the speed of light – and he, Topher, was on its back!

Now the only lights he could see were above him, and he was heading for them. He, Topher, was heading for the stars!

Whoosh! Whoosh!

All he could hear now was the beat of the bird's wings, propelling him forward through dimensions he couldn't name.

Whoosh! Whoosh!

He was going to Ka! He was going to Ka!

He was sure about this, felt it in every part of him and he was filled with joy.

Chapter 13

It was later that doubts set in. Later, as he flew through mile after mile of nothingness, and the stars seemed as far away as ever. What had Old Charlie said – if you travel to the stars you'll come back younger than when you went? Did he want to be younger? Did he want to be a baby? What if he went back further than that – to when he was a *nothing*?

It was a horrific thought. More followed. Was he getting younger? He wished he could see himself? How much younger did he have to be to find Ka – in Bubastis, in Ancient Egypt? Wasn't that *thousands* of years ago? *Who* would he be in Ancient Egypt, for surely he couldn't be a nothing? And where would he be and who with? As the bird flew onward – onward? to the past? – the questions in his mind grew more frenzied. He wanted Ka, yes he did, but didn't he want her on his bed, in the kitchen, or on the front doorstep? Was he going to the past to fetch her back or – horrors! – would he have to stay there for ever? Suddenly, the enormity of what was happening overwhelmed him, and Topher longed for home.

But the falcon was flying even faster it seemed and the wind was sucking at his pyjamas like a vacuum cleaner, and there was something ahead, several some-things. One of them whizzed past him, a lump of molten rock, and the stars did seem nearer. They shone more brightly, and he could see more strange objects, showers of sparks and spheres with fiery tails. Further away he saw the planets circling – and he longed for ordinariness.

He longed for his dad and he longed for Ellie, and he was hurtling away from them. And the wind was colder and stronger now, it seemed to be trying to blast him off the falcon's back. Topher clung on, his arms round the bird's neck, as its wings beat furiously. He was scared now, very scared. He didn't know where he was going, or whether he would ever get back. Icy fear sliced through him.

Then the wind dropped and his pyjama jacket was floating gently, tickling his skin. It was silent again, so silent he could hear his own heart thumping, hear the blood racing through his veins. He forced himself to breathe deeply and slowly, and he could hear the air swooshing through his nostrils, filling his lungs; and his heartbeat slowed as he hoped it would. It was a good trick, which his mum had taught him. He breathed in again and let out his breath slowly, heard his finger joints click as he relaxed his hold on the bird's neck. He breathed in again, slowly, deeply, felt calmer now. He was still afraid but fear wasn't filling him.

Curious too, he wondered where he was. It was getting lighter. He was glad of that even though he wasn't afraid of the dark. He had been when he was younger so maybe he wasn't getting younger. He was glad of that too. Feeling tired, he leaned forward a little, rested his head on the falcon's soft feathers and closed his eyes – just for a moment – but he must have slept, for when he opened his eyes things had changed. It was lighter still, and there was something ahead, a huge luminous ball. It was strange and yet familiar.

It was of course Earth. He had left Earth and he was coming back to Earth, the planet Earth, looking amazingly like the globe in the corner of the classroom at St. Saviour's, except that there was no shelf beneath it, no stand for it to spin on. Then what did it spin on? The colours were different too. It wasn't a faded blue with yellow and green bits and black writing. It was a deep blue, with an even deeper blue showing the land masses, and these were becoming clearer all the time. They were changing colour by the second, because the falcon was in fact *zooming* towards the earth, its wing beats so fast they were a flickering haze in the corner of his eye. And as he looked ahead blue became green became brown with lines appearing and dots. They must have flown in a curve round the other side for now there was more light – from the sun? – and now he could see the continents, sprawling Asia, and coming into view the bulge of Africa – miles of sand and a river on the right-hand side, branching like a tree.

Africa! Of course! He was heading for Africa, getting closer by the second. Egypt was in Africa! And that river like a tree, it was the Nile!

Now, his head felt muzzy as it had once when he'd had gas at the dentist's. And it was dark again. He glanced round. The falcon's wings were trembling with the effort of staying still. The bird was slowing itself, braking, trying to pull itself back. Then on outstretched wings it was descending again – down, down, down – towards a flat rooftop, in a small settlement surrounded by palm trees and flat bare fields. Bump. The bird landed.

'Ker.' It lowered its rump and Topher slid down its tail feathers to a whitewashed roof terrace.

He was in the past; for a few seconds he knew that, knew that he'd left the future behind. He was Topher and he wasn't Topher. He was no longer Topher Hope and he felt very very tired.

Chapter 14

Then he was waking up, as if after deep sleep, rubbing his eyes with one hand, holding a cloth around his middle with another. Through his fingers he could see the streaked dawn sky, purple and indigo with palm trees silhouetted against the horizon. He could hear honking ducks and shrieking ibis, see them if he stood on tiptoe, flocks of them on the flat dark earth. Something was worrying him but he couldn't remember what. He didn't feel quite himself. Frondy leaves tickled his legs. He needed the lavatory. Perhaps that was what it was. He would have to go downstairs.

Making his way to the outside steps he glanced over the wall to the next-door neighbour's house. Nobody there was up yet, not even their noisy children, though Ra the sun god was. A crimson dome on the horizon, he was flooding the dawn sky with pink and gold, making the wet earth shimmer. Already slaves were in the fields. He could hear the plink plink of their wooden hoes, and the high cry of ibis wheeling above them. The recent flood had subsided quite quickly. It had been a good flood, high enough to cover the fields with silt, but not so high as to damage the houses and dykes. There would be a rich harvest. Thanks be to the gods!

He hurried up. What was the matter with him? His stomach ached, always a sign that he was worried about something. Good, here was the lav, next to his parents' quarters. It didn't smell today; the sand beneath the painted seat was fresh. He knew he was lucky to live in a house like this, to have a bed with a mattress and linen sheets. Then why hadn't he slept in his? His parents were important people, that's why they had these things. His father was a scribe, a rich man, and his mother – he didn't know exactly what she did – but she was important too. Sometimes she went away. She had to, she said.

But she was home now, he could see her, through a curtain. He could see both of them in their bed with its feet shaped like lion's paws. They were still asleep, his father's shaved head and his mother's cropped one on their padded headrests.

Why hadn't he slept in his own bed last night?

'Topher, is that you?'

'Yes, Mother.' Her headrest clattered to the floor.

'Why are you up so early, Topher?'

'I don't know.'

'Go back to bed then.'

'Yes, Mother.'

Then she was sitting up, anxious. 'Topher, did you find Ka?'

That was it. He'd been looking for the house cat.

'No, Mother.'

He watched her but didn't let her see him. She would hate that. Without her make-up she looked like a ghost. With make-up her eyes were like a cat's, but now her skin was pale and puffy, with wrinkles at the eye-edges. She was frowning, seemed worried about the house cat, and so of course was he. But not his father, snoring beside her. Now memory returned, and anger rose like sick in his throat. His father, Kris, wasn't worried and yet he *knew*. He was a scribe. He had seen the sacred papyrus.

And Topher knew. *He* had seen the sacred papyrus. The knowledge pressed down on him like a tombstone. He shouldn't have looked, shouldn't have read the hieroglyphs. It had happened yesterday when his father had taken him to his workplace.

'You could be an apprentice scribe one day,' he'd said. 'You could copy out the sacred texts, like me.'

Then he'd been called away, for just a few moments, leaving Topher with *The Secret of Bastet* in front of him – and he'd read it – learned the threat it held for Ka. That's why he'd slept on the roof, he'd been looking for her, wanted to save her.

He glanced through the curtain, saw his mother still in bed, but now putting on her thick black wig. He went in. She held out both hands. He told her he feared Ka had drowned in the mud, or that a hyena had got her.

She shuddered, shook her head, said he mustn't worry, said it again. 'You mustn't worry.' And she stroked his cheek, gently scratching him with her long fingernails.

Was she worried – about Ka? She seemed more worried about him now. Yet she'd adored Ka, and Ka had adored her. Didn't Ka deserve their worry?

'These things happen you know, Topher. It's the will of the gods. You must accept it!' Saying this she looked him straight in the eyes – and he had a terrible thought. Did she know too? He tried to read her face, but she turned away, was getting out of bed. And his father was stirring. Topher saw the two of them exchange a look. It seemed heavy with meaning. Did they both know? He needed to think, but he must watch and listen too. His father was speaking now.

'It can be an . . . honour you know, Topher, to lose the house cat.'

So he had been awake, listening. He went on, 'Besides, no real harm can come to Ka you know. She has the lucky ankh, remember?'

How could he forget? The sacred ankh, the sign of life which adorned her forehead! For as long as he could remember people had always said she was a lucky cat, that she could be the goddess Bastet herself! Poor unlucky Ka!

For he knew exactly what his father meant. He had seen it written down. It could be an honour to lose the house cat if she had been chosen, if she had been taken to the temple of Bubastis. If broken-necked and wearing a cloth of gold she were to be paraded through the streets of Bubastis, to be cheered by the gullible crowds as the goddess Bastet herself.

He had to save Ka from that.

Chapter 15

He couldn't tell anyone. To have read the sacred text was a profanity. Even to think of stopping the sacred rite was to risk death, but he must rescue Ka. He must go to Bubastis. He was sure she was there by now. Who had taken her? She had been missing for a whole day and the festival of Bastet was imminent. That's when she would be killed, on the day of the festival, at sunset.

He went again to the rooftop; he needed to be alone to think.But the children next door were playing in their roof garden. Narma who was four saw him.

'Rrrrrrr!' He was pulling a toy lion which snapped its jaws when he jerked the string. 'Rrrrrrr! Come on over, Topher.'

'No. Sorry.' He felt mean because he was Narma's favourite, a pretend big brother, but he couldn't think with him there. He would have to go downstairs again. Fortunately he went by the outside staircase, for passing his parents' window he heard something which stopped him in his tracks.

Crouching, he listened.

Bubastis! He had heard right. They were going there! Both of them were, though previously only his mother had planned to, but this year, as they had been 'honoured' . . . So they both did know! Topher felt sick – but kept his wits about him – and soon heard something which made his heart thump faster.

'I'm worried about Topher.' That was his mother. 'I think he knows something he shouldn't.'

'What do you mean?'

'You know what I mean.'

'How could he?'

'I don't know, but he's acting oddly. He was too fond of the cat, Kris. Too fond.'

There was a pause, then his father's voice again. 'Maybe we should take him with us? Keep an eye, of course.'

'Don't be stupid!' His mother *hissed*.

Topher's mind raced. They were going to Bubastis. Ka was involved. Then they must take him with them!

Silently, he moved away from the window, crept down the remaining steps – planning. A few moments later, whistling cheerfully, he walked past their door. Slaves were helping them dress.

'Ah, Topher!' His father saw him. 'Here a moment. We're going away tomorrow – to Bubastis.'

Here was his chance – so soon! It was up to him now.

'Oh, can I come? The Feast of Bastet, is it?'

He must sound keen, but give no hint of his real reason for wanting to go. 'Mosi said it was great fun. His parents took him last year. He said the journey was hilarious and the food and drink were fantastic, especially the food.' He laughed. So did they. Mosi was very fat. Then once again they looked at each other excluding him. In the corner of the room the water clock dripped.

His mother, he thought, was shaking her head, but his father was smiling, and seemed to be dismissing her

72

worries. Good.

'Why not?' Kris put his arms around them both. 'It will be a family outing.'

When he'd left the room, Topher raced round to the window again and heard his father say, 'I think you're wrong, Tiy. He didn't even mention the cat just then.'

So far so good. Preparations had already begun – the packing, special foods to take with them – but there was more to do.

His mother said Topher and his father should have new clothes. There was much discussion. Should Topher have a long robe like a man's or a short one like a boy's? A short one, she decided, this year. She put her arm round him, drew him close to her. 'For you must run around and enjoy yourself at the festival. You're still a boy, you know, and you mustn't think so much.'

The robe-maker came with his measuring rod and his rolls of cloth. Topher looked cheerful, and he didn't mention Ka.

But that night he dreamed about her. It was a terrible dream. He failed. He failed to save her, and he cried out with the misery of it.

'I tried to save you, Ka! I tried! I TRIED!'

The cry woke him – and his mother, though at first he didn't recognise her standing by the side of his bed. With her bare head and pale night shift she looked like a ghost.

'What's the matter, Topher?'

He shook his head.

'Tell me.' She knelt by his bed, and touched his cheek – and he longed to tell her but the words wouldn't come.

In the morning he thought he remembered her leaving

his room, and wondered what she had heard. He tried to look cheerful, eager to be off. He *was* eager to be off. Too anxious to eat breakfast, he said he was too excited to eat and his father laughed and said there would be plenty to eat later, but his mother said he should eat something now. His father left the table, but when Topher tried to leave she restrained him, a hand on his.

But she didn't make him eat. She wanted him to promise she said – that when they got to Bubastis he wouldn't do anything *stupid*. On the word 'stupid' she held his gaze with her green cat-eyes, and he said lightly that of course he wouldn't do anything stupid. But that wasn't enough she said, he must promise. So he promised – because what he was going to do, or try to do, wasn't stupid. It was essential. And she seemed pleased, became bright and brisk, hugged him, said she knew he was a sensible boy, and that they must hurry now. The barge it seemed was waiting.

He said, 'Great,' and 'I'm really looking forward to it.' And hoped she couldn't read his mind.

She did keep him close to her as they left the house. She'd been away so much lately, she said. It was so nice to have time to talk to him. He didn't know what to say. Fortunately, once they got into the street he didn't have to say anything. They were joined by so many others, mostly grown-ups, a few families but not many children – all making their way to the river where the barge was waiting. Already they could hear shouts from the small harbour, smell fish and tar. Kris went off quite soon saying he must say hello to old Nakhti. They didn't see him again till they reached the river and he hailed them from the boarding stage.

It was all very jolly and noisy. People were enjoying themselves and Topher found it hard not to despite his fears for Ka. He felt like a traitor, then remembered it was for the best. He ought to look cheerful. His mother was still watching him quite closely.

As they walked onto the barge it dipped and rocked, plunging ibis-headed Thoth and jackal-headed Anubis into the muddy waters, for their images covered the sides, and the black and white eye of Horus glared from the prow. Hapi, the river god, flew from the gaudy sail, a rare god with a human face. The gods were everywhere. The gods decide. Everybody said so. Everybody accepted it. Then why couldn't he?

Because of a cat called Ka.

How much longer before they got going? For a moment his worries came to the fore, then noticing his mother looking at him, he pointed to the strange-looking person in front of them.

'Is it a man or woman?' he mouthed. She shook her head, laughed. He laughed. The barge shook with laughter and his mother pointed out a harpist just boarding, and other musicians. A short while afterwards they started to tune their instruments and a high-pitched voice sang praises to Hapi.

Surely they must set sail soon? He asked his mother. She pointed to slaves on the bank, still holding fast the ropes and to other people only just coming into the harbour.

But at last the latecomers were boarding, lifting their long robes so as not to trip over them, holding onto their elaborate wigs because of the stiff breeze. Laughing loudly, they greeted friends and accepted offers of wine from the huge pitchers which stood at each end of the deck. Surely they were the last? More singers now heaped praise on the river god. The music grew louder. Surely now they were ready?

But the glistening slaves still held fast the ropes, and the gangplank stayed in place. Now the whine of flutes, the clatter of castanets and the raucous shouts of revellers filled Topher's ears, drowning his thoughts. But there was another sound which brought them back to the surface – the wail of cats, calling from baskets and bags, and luckier ones from the ends of leads, for every family aboard seemed to have brought one as a gift to the goddess.

Except one of course. For theirs had gone before.

Ka! Ka! I'm coming to get you.

Topher willed his thoughts to his cat.

'Move along! Move along! Down below some of you, please!' an official roared.

'Come along, Topher.' Grasping his arms, Tiy made her way towards some steps, leading he supposed to cabins below. Then someone thrust a goblet of wine into her hand.

'Tiy!'

'Shery!' Tiy greeted her friend and took a gulp and a few moments later seemed to have forgotten him. Hanging back, he saw her going down the steps, looking over her shoulder, looking for him he supposed, but then the barge lurched, and she was struggling to keep her balance, splashing wine over her friend. He took his chance and headed for the bows.

He wasn't exactly alone. Sailors were busy checking

the sail, but at least he could think, and he could watch the bank. But it seemed ages before the slaves on shore started to unwind the ropes from the bollards, winding them round their arms.

Then 'Look out!' A shout made him step aside – just in time – as a rope came flying and landed near his feet. More followed. Then the overseer roared and the oarsmen behind him heaved.

'One two! One two!

One two! One two!'

Slowly, the barge swung away from the boarding stage.

They were off. He was on his way.

Chapter 16

But how slowly they moved!

The landing stage seemed to inch away. Even the ducks in the reed thickets, disturbed by the wake, seemed to rise in slow motion, land in slow motion, the splashes as they hit the water, rising in slow curves. But eventually ducks and splashes were no longer visible as the barge reached the middle of the river, and with a shout the helmsman strained on the rudder, the oarsmen heaved and the barge swung round to face downstream. It straightened and then there was bank on either side, stretching ahead for as far as Topher could see – miles and miles of featureless bank, and miles and miles of featureless mud beyond them. The sameness was mesmerising.

Moving to the stern for a change of scene, he found a coil of rope to sit on and thought of Ka and how he would rescue her. First he must get inside the temple. That should be quite easy. Then he must give his parents the slip. That too was possible. He'd proved it already. How long had he got? That was the key question. He must find Ka before sunset. Already the sun was high in the sky. It was getting hotter and the wind had dropped. Doing nothing, that was the difficult bit.

He watched the v of the wake become wider and wider, disappear. He watched it again, widen, disappear. He watched a hippopotamus slide into the water, slide, disappear. And reappear, its eyes above the water near the boat – and he stood up, suddenly alert to danger! It could upturn the boat and they could all drown.

'Don't worry.' A laughing girl was by his side, pointing to a group of men with throw-sticks and spears who had also suddenly appeared. But throw-sticks and spears – against a thick-skinned hippopotamus? Now the men were shouting at it and making threatening gestures. 'See,' said the girl. 'It's going!' He hoped she'd go too, then changed his mind. It might be better if she stayed, and stopped him thinking so much. For wasn't the hippo supposed to be a goddess too? Wasn't she Taweret, the goddess of fertility? So why were those men ready to kill her, with everyone's approval presumably? It didn't make sense.

'What are you thinking about?' The girl said her name was Amet.

'Nothing.' For what could he say? Nobody else seemed to think like him.

'Let's go below then.' She pulled him by the arm. 'It's fun down there.' He followed but couldn't stop thinking. What about Ka? Was she a goddess, or simply a cat he loved? Was the hippo a goddess or a wild animal? Now Amet was opening the cabin door. Noise burst out and hot air hit him like a flannel. Amet dived into the fray, but Topher had seen enough – his father for a start, perfume dripping down his nose.

He found his old spot near the helmsman, who fortunately didn't say anything. He just stared into the distance his hand on the rudder. There were no passengers here either, and the oarsmen behind him concentrated on rowing, unfaltering as ever but slower now he was sure. How long would it take to reach Bubastis? Would he be in time? Ra was overhead now. It must be midday. The sun god ruled. Would they get there before sunset? They must.

'Here.' Oh no. It was Amet again, her wig skew-whiff. 'You're not much fun, are you? I thought you were coming below.' She gave him a goblet of wine. The thick liquid burned his throat, seemed to make his thoughts come quicker, dangerous blasphemous thoughts.

If Ka were a goddess, why *break her neck*?

If the hippo were a goddess, why kill it?

If Ka *were* a goddess, why *pretend* she was a goddess?

'Look out, stupid.' Amet was pulling him away, saving him from the elbows of the helmsman who was straining on the rudder now, swinging the barge towards the shore. For a moment his hopes rose. Had they arrived? No. It was only a village, Amet explained. Couldn't he see the villagers holding their oxen or leaning on their hoes? And here, she said, the fun really began. She was giggling already, watching the cabin door. He knew what was going to happen. Mosi had told him. A few seconds later the door burst open and a line of drunken grown-ups emerged from below. Noisy, staggering they were like a giant snake each hanging on to the one in front, and soon the snake was coiling round the deck. Then, suddenly, it disintegrated as they all raised their arms and clapped, then turned, bent over and 'mooned' to the people on the shore.

Topher went below, hoping to find his parents there, hoping they weren't with the idiots above, but no, the cabin was empty except for a few cats, mewing loudly now from their baskets. He sat down on a wine-soaked bench. Perhaps he should rest, keep his strength for the task ahead. He closed his eyes and must have fallen asleep, for when he opened them the barge was lurching to one side and his father was peering into the cabin.

'Come on, Topher. We're at Bubastis. You must stay by me now.' Up on deck people were jostling for places in the papyrus boats which would take them from the barge to the shore. Some had crossed the stretch of water already and were clambering out on the other side. A few were making their way past the net menders and fish sellers, up the track to the temple.

It stood on a hill, dominating the harbour and the town. It looked like a fort, solid and impenetrable. On the side facing the river there were no doors or even windows, but as he lowered himself into the flimsy boat, Topher willed a message to Ka. I'm close to you now, Ka. I'm coming to save you. He would get into the temple somehow.

Chapter 17

There was an entrance, magnificent bronze doors on the west front, and crowds were climbing the several flights of steps which led to them.

'Let's go!' Topher didn't have to fake his eagerness to see them close up. Surely he could give his parents the slip later. But his father's hand gripped his arm.

'No.' He was shaking his head, seemed amused.

'Why not?' Topher tried to pull away. The sooner he got to the top the better. Several people were there already, might even be inside.

'Why not?' he repeated.

'Well look,' said Kris, almost laughing now.

Topher looked – at the doors and the pointed obelisks either side of them, at the gigantic statue of Bastet above the doors and the crowds going up to worship her. 'What is it?' he said, for still Kris held his arm. 'Why can't we go?'

'Can't you see?' Kris was laughing now. 'It's women only, stupid! Only your mother can go inside the temple.'

It took a few seconds for his words to sink in, but then Topher saw that the crowd at the foot of the steps was in fact dividing, with women going one way, men the other. And it was only women, going up the hill with their cats.

'So you come with me,' said Kris. 'We men can watch the procession together.' The 'we men' was supposed to flatter him.

'I don't want to.'

Now he saw that glance pass between his father and mother again, excluding him. He saw his father shrug.

'I want to go with Mother.'

'You can't.'

'I want to.'

He sounded like a baby; he knew that. I want my mummy. I want my mummy. Tiy looked upset.

Kris was annoyed and suddenly Topher thought his arm was being wrenched from its socket as Kris said, 'You'll see her later!' and started to drag him away. It took all Topher's wits to stay on his feet and try and keep track of where he was going as his father zig-zagged through dusty streets and alleyways. He didn't stop till they reached a crowded square. It had taken them several minutes to get there.

'I'm sorry about that, Topher, but you were making a fool of yourself – and me.' He looked round as if worried that people might still be watching them, then loosening his grip, said, 'What would you like to do now?'

'I don't know yet.'

Topher looked over his shoulder, still determined to escape. The temple was still visible – at least the statue of Bastet was. He thought he could make his way back to it. Taking his bearings he hoped he looked as if he were thinking about his father's question. There were houses on all sides of the square. Several streets led off it. Sellers were bawling out their wares. One came up to them, tried to garland them with lotus blossom. Another urged them to taste his honey comb. Topher watched it all, especially his father and he waited.

His father was greeting an old friend now. In the far corner there was a crowd round a storyteller, and in the side street opposite a chained bear was dancing. And now Kris was buying his old friend a drink from a water carrier. Watching him, Topher edged towards the nearest side street, and found himself looking at a stall on the corner. It was full of cats. There were hundreds of them, not real cats, but models, rows and rows of them on a striped cloth.

'Buy a lucky cat, young fellow.'

The seller was a Bedouin from the desert. He had a beard, and more striped cloth round his middle.

'Come on, buy a lucky cat.' He held out a blue one. It was made of lapis lazuli. Topher liked it, but there was another he liked better at the back of the stall if liked was the word. He couldn't take his eyes off this cat. Made of reddish gold stone, with waves of white and flecks of black it seemed to shine – and it was the image of Ka!

'Ah. Special, that one,' said the Bedouin, following his gaze. 'It's sardonyx you see, from Ratanpur in India.'

He picked it up and held it out, and the cat looked at Topher.

Hurry Topher, hurry.

A talking cat! How did it do it? He wondered if the Bedouin was some sort of ventriloquist.

Hurry!

Could he, could he leave now and make his way to the temple? He glanced back at his father – and caught his eye. Curses! Kris was watching him. Topher turned back to the Bedouin, and the cat on his hand shone even brighter.

'*Help me, Ka. You've got to help me.*'

He didn't realise he had spoken aloud, or that the Bedouin had been paying such close attention. So, when a few moments later there was an uproar behind him, and the Bedouin said, 'Here's your chance,' he was taken by surprise. He turned to see what the commotion was about and saw his father with a baboon on his head! It was tugging at his wig – and a crowd had gathered. People were shouting and laughing.

'Now's your chance!' hissed the Bedouin, and Topher ran.

He knew the direction because the temple was never out of sight. Ra, the sun god, was still high in the sky, but dropping visibly. As he got closer it dropped again and the statue of Bastet became a silhouette against a reddening sky.

How long had he got? How long before sunset? He ran without stopping, despite a stitch in his side, and at last he came to the foot of the steps – and ran past them, for there was something he must do first.

A few minutes later – wearing a shift and a wig stolen from a girl bathing in the river – he began the climb to the temple.

He went as fast as he could. There was no point in trying to look inconspicuous. He just hoped he looked enough like a girl. No one else was going up. Only a few women were coming down. As he got nearer he could see a few round the door quite clearly; he saw that in fact they were in front of a smaller door within

the huge one, and the small door was opening and closing. Things were being passed in. Cats! Of course! The
gifts for the goddess. Then why had his mother gone up
to the temple? Her cat had gone before her. Now he
could hear a cat mewling, could see a bald-headed figure
reaching out to take it, reaching out again to give back
an empty basket.

Then the door closed and stayed closed. Was he too
late?

Three women started to walk down the hill, and
Topher passing them on the way up, glanced across,
wondering for a second if one of them could be his
mother. None of them was.

Now he was alone and the nearness of everything
concentrated his mind. As he heaved himself up the last
few steps he went over his plan.

The sky above was purple now. From inside the building he heard a sound of rattling drums. Had the ceremony begun? He banged on the door.

'Let me in! Let me in!'

I have an urgent message, he planned to say, for the
high priestess herself and I must deliver it personally.
That would get him close to Ka surely.

Nobody answered.

And now sound drowned thought, for from behind
the doors came more rattling, a crash of cymbals and
the wail of a thousand cats. Now he pounded on the
door, though it seemed useless, for who could hear
above that racket? He pounded the door till his knuckles
hurt and he cried out.

'I have an urgent message for the high priestess herself! Let me in!'

The door remained shut. And now he noticed ears on the door, carvings of human ears. They were on either side of a prayer to Bastet, and they seemed to mock him as he read the words.

'Hear me, o goddess,
Bastet, queen of the night,
Lead me to your shrine.'

'Yes, Ka, lead me to your shrine before it's too late.'

He knocked again with the palms of his hands, but no ears were listening, or perhaps they were, for after a few minutes he realised the caterwauling had stopped and he thought he heard something clatter on the other side of the door. A bolt being drawn back? A spy-hole perhaps? But no one opened the door. He couldn't see very well because it was nearly dark. Surely the sun had set? He thought he could see a star in the sky.

From the town below sounds rose, voices, music, the clink of cooking vessels and the smell of roasting meat. His parents would be looking for him now. Could they see him up here, a single figure knocking at a door? He may as well go and find them, but first he had better take off these girls' clothes. As he turned away and went to pull the shift over his head he thought of Ka inside the building. I've failed you, Ka, I've failed you. Sorry.

Then he felt hands grabbing him.

Chapter 18

'Spy!'

'Spy!'

'We have been watching you, spying!'

The two priestesses spoke together in weird sing-song voices. They looked weird too with their bald heads and long black robes streaked like a cat's fur. Topher was in trouble, but at least he was in trouble inside the temple and fortunately they still thought he was a girl; they had dragged him in before he'd removed the shift.

'Well, now you must stay here.'

'For ever!'

A girl! For ever! He hoped not, but hoped too that they couldn't read his thoughts. His hand rose to his wig. It had stayed in place, but for how long? Would they take it off, shaving his head like theirs? He could see the veins in their gleaming white skulls. On the wall a torch flickered. From behind it came the rhythmic beat of chanting. He could make out a name now.

'Tababua! Tababua!'

The priestesses stared at him.

'You want to see the high priestess?'

'See Tababua perform the sacred rite?'

'Join our sisterhood?'

He nodded eagerly, for he must see Ka.

They consulted.

'We should bathe her first.'

'Cleanse and purify.'

It was a moment of pure horror! Surely now he was done for!

But then – 'She looks clean enough.'

'She's a pretty girl.'

He breathed again and they stroked his cheeks with golden claws.

'What's your name, pretty girl?'

'Meu.'

'A goodly name for one of our calling. But hark.'

The chanting next door rose to a crescendo.

'TABABUA!

TA-BA-BU-A!'

Then silence.

'We can enter now. There is a pause in the ceremony.'

One priestess opened the door, signalling him to follow. The other closed the door and he found himself behind a pillar in a shadowy hall. Here and there candles flickered. The hall was empty he thought, but then the chanting began again and he noticed black heaps on the floor. The chanting was coming from them, louder now as they raised their white skulls, then more softly as they lowered them again, softer still as they spread themselves over the floor. The chanting was now a murmur. Something nudged Topher's ankle. It was the priestess by his side, now face down on the floor, signalling that he should do the same. And he did so, joining in, striving to make his voice match theirs.

'Tababua. Tababua.'

'Tababua! Tababua!'

Louder and louder the voices grew, and faster and

faster, till with a shout the priestesses rose to their feet, begging the high priestess to appear before them.

And suddenly there she was – a giantess looking down on them! Tababua herself! Perhaps she had been there all the time hidden by the darkness, but now a circle of torches revealed her splendour, her headdress a whole peacock's tail, her robe a cascade of blue. But something else caught Topher's eye – in her raised right hand a gold sickle, in her left held high a little cat. She had it by the scruff of the neck, exposing its white throat – and as he watched the sickle flashed.

'NO!' He rushed forward.

'NO!' He pulled off his white shift and girl's wig.

The cat dropped from her hand.

'I'm a boy!'

'*Boy!*'

There was a gasp, then a deathly silence – except for a stirring at the far side, a whisper of garments as a figure disappeared through a door, to summon guards perhaps. But nothing happened, till suddenly hands grabbed him. A boy! Horror! He had violated the sacred rite, polluted the temple. What must they do? They looked to their leader.

Tababua glared down at him.

Topher trembled. This surely was the end. But he *had* saved Ka! It was Ka. He had seen the ankh on her forehead before she shot away. He prayed that she had escaped.

'Bear him to me!' Tababua had spoken.

Now hands grabbed his wrists and ankles, hoisted him high, and he was carried to the foot of the dais – horizontal like a sacrifice.

'He shall not leave these walls alive. His punishment is Death.'

Above him the curved blade of the sickle glittered. Terror froze him as the high priestess raised her arm. So this was it.

The arm descended and he closed his eyes.

Then, 'NO!'

A voice boomed.

Cymbals clashed.

And he was on his feet again, his eyes open – for he had been dropped. All eyes were facing the back of the hall – where in a long saffron robe, stood a huge cat, the sacred ankh on her forehead, the ring in her left ear and the eye of Horus round her neck.

'Bastet! Bastet!'

A whisper went round the hall. The goddess had come among them! The priestesses fell to their knees, gazing with awe as they broke into a prayer.

'Bastet, Bastet,
How manifold are all thy works.
Bastet, Bastet.
They are hidden before us.
Bastet, Bastet,
O goddess whose powers
No other possesseth.
Bastet!
Queen of the Night!'

Never before had the goddess herself appeared before them.

'You dare to look at me!'

She spoke and overcome, they hid their faces. And

now she pointed at Topher.

'Spoiler of my rites, approach!'

Slowly he walked forward.

'Desecrater of my temple. Closer!'

He stepped forward and her arms opened wide, the saffron robes shimmering like a sheet of flame before him. Then the voice boomed again, from the cat mouth above him.

'Male-child, you have violated my sacred rite.
Your sight disgusts me.
At my command you will leave this life
To wander alone in the void!
ZAZAMANKA!'

Cymbals clashed as her hands came together and silky folds gathered round him. To those few who dared watch it looked as if he had been consumed by flames. One moment he was there, the next he had vanished. To Topher inside it all it felt like dying, smothering in the silky folds tightening round his head and body. Then suddenly he found he could breathe again, and from somewhere in the dark folds he heard whispered commands.

'Topher, I'm going to turn round now, and you must turn too. I shall open my arms and you will see a door before you. Go through it.'

He thought he recognised the voice, but there was no time to think.

'ZAZAMANKA!'

The goddess boomed again, and she was turning round, and he was turning, and she was opening her arms, releasing him, and there was a door on the back wall in front of him.

Now the whispering voice again, more urgent now. 'Go, Topher! You'll find everything you need beyond the door. Quickly, go! Move, it's your only chance.'

'ZA-ZA-MAN-KA!'

She turned from him towards the hall and her adoring acolytes, and he moved, through the door which opened as he approached and closed after him. He found himself in a small room, a table before him, and on the table was a papyrus scroll. It was a map of the temple, and marked on it clearly was a secret exit, and the words, 'Go, with your mother's blessing.'

So he was right. It was his mother! Suddenly he understood – everything. She was a priestess. This is where she used to come. She was one of the priesthood, one of the trusted few. But she was betraying that trust now, pretending to be the goddess – to save his life. From the other side of the door her goddess-voice boomed.

'Sisters.'

The priestesses responded. 'Bastet, revered Bastet!' She continued,

> 'In the streets below
> The people await us,
> Lead me to them.'

He thought he heard bolts being drawn back, the scrape of huge doors opening, the sluther of shuffling feet. She was making it easy for him and she had told him to go with her blessing. He could go. There was a passage leading from the room he was in – his escape route. But what about Ka? That's who he'd come for. Where was she? His mother had said nothing about Ka. Could he risk looking out? Could he risk looking for Ka?

It took him several minutes to find the mechanism which opened the door, and as it slid back he looked out nervously. Waited. When no one appeared he crept out. Then slowly, quietly he felt his way forward, till he was crouching behind the dais on which his mother had stood. His mother! He wished he had time to think. She must have suspected his plan all along? How well she knew him, but how had she managed to trick everyone else? What a risk she was taking! The hall was dark. A single torch burned where Tababua had stood. Opening the huge doors must have blown the rest of them out. The doors were still slightly open. The hall was shadowy, seemed empty but he couldn't be sure. Someone could easily be hiding behind a pillar.

He wanted to call out but dared not. Ka, where are you?

But then came a cry from a ledge high above him.

'Mwa!'

He looked up.

'Mwa! Mwaaa!'

And there was Ka, a silhouette against the torchlight, her long tail quivering. She seemed distressed, and as he watched he saw why. The shelf on which she stood was crumbling.

Chapter 19

She leaped – and landed on her feet! Of course. Only
a cat could, only a cat like Ka! One second she was
stuck on a ledge, crying piteously, the next she was
flying through the air like an acrobat. Then she was
purring rapturously, rubbing against his legs, loosening
clouds of dust so thick he could hardly see the lines and
flecks of her beautiful golden fur. He bent to stroke her.

'We must go, Ka.'

'Mwa. Mwaaa!'

First, he had to follow her. She led him to a door
from behind which came a mournful mewing. When he
opened it a sea of cats rushed out, wave after wave of
them nearly knocking him off his feet. Past him they
swept and through the huge door and down the hill. He
thought Ka might join them but she stayed with him,
watching them. He thought he might join them, take his
chance in the town below, but then he remembered his
mother's commands.

Ka followed him. Through the secret door they went,
then into the passage as his mother had instructed. It
was dark and narrow, a tunnel really. He had to crawl,
clutching the map which he hoped he'd memorised, for
it was too dark to read. For Ka, moving at least was
easier. Sometimes she ran ahead of him, but came back
frequently to check he was coming. He felt her against

his arms or legs, or thought he did. At times the dust was so thick it felt a bit like fur, and his shoulders rubbing against the tunnel walls made more dust. It was hard to breathe. He wished he had something to tie over his nose and mouth.

But he kept on – there was no choice – feeling his way forward, feeling with his right hand for a turning to the right, which he was sure the map instructed him to take. His hands and knees felt sore now, and his toes. How much longer? The map hadn't indicated distances. That was a problem. He urged himself on. If he took the turning to the right he would eventually come to three doors the map said. But where was this turning? He stopped for a moment, felt the wall to his right, felt wall and more wall as far as he could reach. No turning. Had he missed it? He started to crawl again.

Then he had to stop, for Ka was nudging his forehead. No, more than nudging – she was trying to push him backwards. He could feel her skull against his.

'Get out of the way, Ka.'

Rrrrrr. Rrrrrr. She was growling at him, sounded like a wild cat!

'Ouch!'

She had scratched him. He backed off, felt stickiness on his cheek. It was so unlike her.

'Why, Ka?'

Now she was purring. 'So..rrrrry. So..rrrrry.' Then the purr changed and she was nudging him again. 'Rrrrre . . . verse. Rrrrrre . . . verse,' she seemed to say.

'In a minute, Ka.'

For he had been thinking, wanted to try something.

She didn't want him to, yowled as he lay flat on the tunnel floor, stretching his arm as far as it would reach. When he shuffled a few centimetres forward she bit his shoulder, tried to tug him backwards – and a few seconds later he realised why. Beneath his fingertips was dry crumbling mud. Then nothing at all.

He picked up a small lump of mud, threw it, waited for it to drop. Heard nothing. He shuffled back.

'Thanks, Ka.' She was close to his face. He rubbed it against her fur. What a miraculous creature she was. There was a chasm ahead. If she hadn't warned him he'd have dropped to his death. But now what? Was the right turn, their escape route, beyond that crevasse? Had the path fallen away only recently? Then how were they going to get out?

'Mwow!' Ka was in front of him again, nudging his forehead, pushing him backwards.

'I suppose you're right.'

They would have to go back to the temple, take their chance, hope that they could escape while the priestesses were still parading through Bubastis. They would have to find somewhere else to live, where no one knew either of them, a different country perhaps.

And so with Ka gently nudging him if he stopped, he crawled backwards; there wasn't room to turn round. He crawled for perhaps twenty cubits until he realised that Ka had gone, that he hadn't heard or felt her for several seconds. He certainly hadn't seen her. Then he heard a faint mewing. It was coming from his right. He stuck his hand out – and felt nothing! Lowered it and felt a floor. Moved to the left and right and felt walls. Ka had found the turning to the right!

'Mwow!' She was louder now.

'I'm coming, Ka.'

He must have missed it the first time. Now he accelerated, and crashed into something solid. It was a step. There was a flight of them leading upwards, and at the top was a light. And Ka! – her tail quivering like a black flame. She was urging him to hurry.

He hurried, and as he climbed it became lighter, till he reached the top and found himself facing three doors. Above each was a torch. On each one was a word.

Past. Present. Future.

How strange. They all had keys. Which one should he go through? Ka was weaving figures of eight around his legs.

'Which one, Ka?'

She didn't answer. He remembered the map in his hand, read his mother's message.'Go with my blessing,' she had written and also, 'You choose.'

Chapter 20

He chose the future, with all its uncertainty, because he thought he heard someone calling him.

Opening the door, he found himself gulping cool air as he gazed at the night sky. It was a deep deep blue splashed with huge white stars, haloed with turquoise. Light poured from them, flooding the flat temple roof. Ka was by his side. He and she were tiny, not much bigger than the red claws in front of them, the red claws of Horus the falcon. His black and white eyes looked down on them.

'Ker. Ker.' His hooked beak opened and closed.

'Get on my back. Get on my back.' He seemed impatient, turned so that his tail feathers faced them. Ka leaped on from the side. Topher clambered up the ladder-tail and as he reached the top, it see-sawed up tipping him into the hollow of the falcon's back. Ka was already there. Topher put his arms round her and the bird stiffened, strode to the roof edge.

Far below them, a trail of ants moved slowly between heaps of mud – the procession moving through the city of Bubastis. Dust clouds made it hard to see the crowd lining the route, but Topher thought he could see them and another trail moving swiftly down the hill – the cats escaping from the temple. And he thought he could hear the crowds cheering Bastet, cheering his mother at the head of the procession. His mother! Would he ever understand what had been going on?

Now, he thought he heard something else – his own name again.

'Topher! Topher!'

Was that his mother? Did she want him? But she had written, 'Go with my blessing.' He had the papyrus in his hand. She had saved his life and told him to choose – and he had chosen the future.

He looked up, to the stars as big as lanterns, and beyond them to the myriads like shiny dust.

'Topher! Topher!'

That voice again – compelling him from – where? And the falcon was flexing its wings now, rocking its passengers.

'I'm coming. I'm coming.'

Feeling the thrust of take-off, he clung to Ka and the falcon soared. Then temple and town were far below. Landing stage, boats and buildings fell away. Ant-like figures became dots then disappeared completely. Then they were over the desert, a giant piece of papyrus, the Nile delta a hieroglyph on its surface, fading . . . as he flew towards the stars.

Chapter 21

'What on earth are you doing?'

He was climbing in, through his bedroom window, and his father was watching him from the doorway.

'I heard something, on the roof. I thought it might be Ka.'

'So?'

'I went to see.'

'Couldn't you just have opened the window?'

'No.'

'Well, was it?'

'Who?'

'Ka.'

'No. I mean yes.'

His father sighed. 'Where is she then?'

Topher was already searching the room. He was sure Ka had come in with him.

'Topher, look at me.' His father's eyes were steely small. 'I'm not sure I believe you. Have you been anywhere else?'

'Dressed like this?' He was in his pyjamas. 'Stealing you mean? Removing owls from gateposts? Flying around with them perhaps?' He got into bed, hoped he'd find Ka under the duvet.

'You're not funny, Topher.'

Ka wasn't under the duvet.

'By the way Mrs Wentworth's been on the phone. I came to tell you earlier but you were asleep.'

It was hard to concentrate on what his father was saying. Where was Ka now? What had happened to his mother in Egypt? There was so much going on in his head. But it seemed Ellie had had her operation.

'She came round from the anaesthetic a few hours ago and she's been asking for you. I'll take you tomorrow if you like.'

Ellie had been asking for him? Had it been Ellie's voice calling him back? Again, he saw himself standing before those three doors – wondering which one to choose, past, present or future. Till he'd heard a voice, her voice?

Then he must go to her. Now. He got out of bed.

'Don't be daft. Do you know what time it is? We'll go tomorrow afternoon. I'll get some grapes.'

But it wasn't that late, only half past eleven. His dad went downstairs and Topher followed. If he couldn't see Ellie, at least he could talk to her family, and he could see if Ka was downstairs. The Wentworths never went to bed early, but he was surprised when Russell answered the phone. Russell the Brussel was giggly with happiness because Ellie was all right. He'd been scared she would die under the anaesthetic, he said.

'So was I.'

'Mum said you should have heard her coming round. She was swearing, and shouting your name at the top of her voice. Said it's a wonder you didn't hear her.'

'I did.'

Russell laughed even more. Topher didn't try to explain. Nobody would believe what had happened that night. He could hardly believe it himself. Russell said it was going to be awful, not knowing for a whole month whether the operation had worked. They'd have to try and help Ellie through it. Topher said he'd do his best. Then his dad appeared and tried to send him to bed.

But he went to the kitchen. Ka wasn't there. She wasn't anywhere in the house as far as he could see. Strange. As he looked, thoughts about the past vied with those of the present, and the present won. Ellie won. He must help her all he could. For a start she would want to talk about the operation, not pretend she wasn't worried. He understood that. One of the bad things about his mum dying was that no one wanted to talk about it. And Ellie said the worst thing about being deaf was that most people couldn't be bothered to talk to her any more. He enjoyed talking to her – you could be honest with Ellie – but he wanted to give her something as well, to make her feel better. What? She'd probably have tons of grapes.

She managed a smile the next day, though she looked awful, all on her own in a side ward. Her head was covered with bandages and there were wires and tubes everywhere and screens that bleeped with mesmerising zig-zag lines. He gave her the flame coloured scarf which had been wrapped round the sardonyx cat, his mother's scarf. Ellie held it against her nose.

'It's lovely. I'll sniff it when I can't stand the hospital smell any longer.'

But she was too tired to say much, and he didn't know what to say to her. So much for his good intentions. He wanted to say, 'Ka's gone.' But it didn't seem right to load her with his worries. So he said, 'How's things?'

and she said, 'Fine,' but they weren't. Her face was pale and still and everything was too clean, and the zig-zag lines and the bleeps kept drawing his attention away from her. And not talking about Ka seemed to stop him talking about anything. He found himself glancing at the clock above her head – and she noticed.

'Don't worry. It's this place. How's Ka?'

'Still gone.'

'She'll be back.'

He longed to tell her about everything that had happened – and why he had his doubts – so why couldn't he?

'She'll be back I said!' For a moment it was the old Ellie speaking, emphasising every word, her face so expressive that it made anyone else's seem blank. 'And this operation is going to work, and everything will be all right!'

Next time he went she was sitting up, with the scarf round her head, over the bandages, with the ends hanging down. She caught hold of them. 'See, I can still sniff it when I need to.'

He could smell the scent too. It brought back memories, of the day his mum had discovered anybody could buy a scarf like it, from the shop in the British Museum. She'd been furious. She'd shouted a lot and he'd been a bit scared, but his dad had laughed, then she'd laughed, and he'd joined in.

'But why?' Ellie didn't understand. 'Why was she furious?'

'Because she liked to be different. She wanted to be the only one with a scarf like that.'

'Is that why she called you Topher?'

'Sort of.'

'You are different, Topher. Unique, I'd say.'

'In some ways. And in some ways not.'

How could he explain – about doubles and things? He didn't really understand it himself.

One afternoon, he said, 'Ellie? What do you think about reincarnation?' – because that was one of the things he'd been thinking about, but that didn't get them very far. The trouble was her hearing was even worse now. She said it would be better after MT Day and when he looked blank she shouted.

'Microphones and Transmitter day! When I'll be able to hear well enough to have philosophical discussions!'

How could he have forgotten? It was ringed in red on a calendar by her bed, the day when the doctors connected the receiver in her head with a microphone and transmitter. Then they'd know whether the operation worked or not. He tried to look optimistic. Failed. She thumped him.

'Honestly, Topher, how many times do I have to tell you? This operation is going to work and Ka will come back!'

'Hope so.'

'That's right, Topher, HOPE!'

He did, and when he got home Ka was on the doorstep!

Chapter 22

His dad said, 'I told you so,' though he hadn't, not for ages. Ka rippled with delight as Topher stroked her, made soft chirruping sounds in her throat. Her fur crackled, clinging to the palm of his hand. She was alive with electricity, winding herself in and out of his legs till his dad had the door open when she sprang inside, and through the hall to the kitchen. Then she doubled back and nuzzled Topher again. But she was very hungry, leaped onto the draining board as soon as they were in the kitchen, and started nudging a tin of Whiskas towards the edge.

'Be patient.'

She could hardly wait for him to open it; and nearly caught her whiskers between the opener and the tin. But hungry as she was, if he moved a step away she followed him, left her dish to rub against his foot. So he had to stay by her side. Close. She was even more beautiful than he remembered. Her fur was glossy – and glossiest of all was the black ankh on her forehead, the ancient sign of life.

He didn't ask her where she had been. There was no need. But when they were in his bedroom, when he was in bed sitting with his back against the pillow and she was on his chest purring like a tractor, he looked into her amber eyes and spoke to her.

'You saved my life, Ka.'

'And you saved mine.'

'Are you going to leave me again, Ka?'

'Never.'

He put out the light and she purred him to sleep.

'Neve..rrrrrrrrrr. Neve..rrrrrrrrr. Neve..rrrrrrrr.'

It was Ellie who noticed that the sardonyx cat had gone, Ellie, whose operation was very successful. In the excitement of her recovery and Ka's return Topher hadn't realised the stone cat had disappeared. Ellie noticed the first time she came round after MT day.

'Your room's a tip, Topher. Where's the Egyptian cat that used to be beside your bed?'

They searched for it, tidying his room in the process, which put his dad in a good mood when he came home from work – till Topher mentioned the missing cat when he looked quite upset.

'When did you see it last?'

'The night I went out on the roof to let Ka in. The night you thought I was out stealing gateposts.'

Fortunately that little mystery had been cleared up.

'You didn't tell me about that, Topher.' Ellie's hearing was much better! She could hear sounds that she couldn't hear before and she was having sessions with a speech therapist that were helping her make sense of them.

'Well, if it was there then, Topher, and if you haven't taken it out of this room it must still be here, somewhere.' His dad's faith in order and logic was still one hundred per cent.

'We have searched pretty thoroughly, Mr Hope.'

Topher's dad didn't answer at first. He was staring at

107

the scarf round Ellie's head.

'Perhaps he gave it to you then, with everything else.'

'Everything? I don't understand.'

'He means the scarf.'

Topher stared at his dad who looked really odd. His face had gone into a sort of spasm. At first he thought he was having a fit. Then he saw he was blinking madly and gulping as if he were holding back tears. He was holding back tears, but only just.

'T-Tessa's scarf.' He left the room.

Ellie took the scarf off. Topher thought he knew what had happened. It must have reminded his dad of his mum, he said, stirring up feelings that he tried to keep hidden.

'I'll go home,' said Ellie.

'No, stay. It'll be all right.'

His dad's bedroom door was closed but not locked, and his dad was face down on the bed. Topher touched his shoulder.

'I miss her, Dad, too.'

He thought the great shuddering sobs would never stop, his dad's or his own, but they did and then they talked – about his mum – and later Ellie appeared with three mugs of tea. Ka was with her. She jumped on the bed and padded from Topher to his dad and back again licking their salty faces with her rough tongue. It tickled and they all laughed a lot. Then Ellie said they really did have to keep the scarf. She looked a bit lop-sided because her hair was still long on one side, short on the other, but she said it was only right that they had something which reminded them so vividly of Mrs Hope.

'After all,' she added, 'if you feel bad about it, you

could buy me another from the British Museum. I've nothing against doubles.'

'Nor have I,' said Topher scratching the top of Ka's head.

They went to the British Museum the next Sunday afternoon. Sylvia came too. She was one of the 'things' they'd talked about. I need friends too, his dad had said. I miss your mum, that's why. He said he'd tried to talk to Topher about her, but got the impression Topher didn't want to know – which was true. There had been a wall between them, which both of them had helped to build. But things looked better now.

They went to the museum in Sylvia's red and white 2CV, which was a bit bumpy but quite good fun, better than the tube anyway. It was a sunny, blustery day and they had the roof open, and could see the pigeons flying about and clouds scudding by.

When they got to the museum Mr Hope gave Topher and Ellie money for a guide book – and a scarf for Ellie – and arranged to meet them at half past four. He and Sylvia went off to look at Prehistoric and Roman Britain. Topher and Ellie wanted to look at Egyptian things. But first there was something Topher had to do.

He had been clutching a heavy book since they'd left the house, trying to make it look inconspicuous. But when they were on their own – well, as on their own as they could be in the entrance hall of the British Museum in August – Ellie said, 'What've you brought that for then? You've been hanging on to it as if it were the crown jewels.'

And he'd frowned; he didn't want to tell her – yet. It wasn't that he liked having secrets from Ellie, quite the opposite, but he needed to check something first.

So he went to the main desk and asked if he could speak to an expert on Ancient Egypt. The lady assistant asked why and he said that he had something Egyptian to ask about. She went into a huddle with a young man assistant, then she came back and asked his name. Then they went into another huddle, then the young man went off – to fetch Miss Davenport, the lady assistant said. Miss Davenport was the Egyptologist.

'What is it? What have you got in there?' Ellie was beside herself with curiosity.

'I've come to find out.'

It was half truth. He knew what he had inside the book, but he needed someone else to tell Ellie. Fortunately Miss Davenport arrived almost immediately. She didn't look like an expert. She had very short red hair and nearly black lipstick, but she was friendly and said her name was Jo-Anne. She had an American accent.

'What can I do for you then?'

'I've got a map and I wondered how old it was.'

'Let's see it then.'

Topher opened the book and there it was – except that it wasn't – wasn't a map that is.

Since he'd last looked at it, all the markings had disappeared. He felt sick. Now, no one would believe him.

'Papyrus,' Miss Davenport was saying, 'it looks quite old.'

'There was a map on it, and some writing.'

She looked at him, hard, and then said, 'Follow me.' They followed her down to the laboratories in the basement of the museum, into a dark room, where she again opened the book and put the bare papyrus under an ultra-violet light. And there was the map again – with the secret route and the message in hieroglyphics!

'Wowsers and double wowsers! Where did you get this?' It was very old, she said.

It was in fact two thousand five hundred years old give or take a few years. They learned this later after tiny fragments had been radiocarbon dated and that it was written in extract of iron and gall berries.

That afternoon, they simply had Jo-Anne Davenport's hunch that it was very old indeed. When she asked again, 'Where did you get this?' Topher said, 'My mother gave it to me.'

And Jo-Anne looked puzzled. Then she said, 'What did you say your name was?'

'Topher Hope.'

'Are you Tessa Hope's son? Professor Hope, the Egyptologist.'

Topher nodded and she whistled then muttered something about being sorry.

'She must have meant to give this to us, before she . . . er . . .'

'Died,' said Topher. 'Yes.'

He told Ellie the real story as they walked around the Egyptian rooms, looking at cats and falcons, baboons and giant pharoahs, and hundreds of mummies and coffins. Ellie liked the toy cat with crystal eyes whose jaw opened showing bronze teeth when you pulled it along. Topher told her his neighbour, Narma, had one.

'It must have been fun being a child in 200 BC,' she said reading the plaque.

'Or even a cat,' she said. They were in front of the

case of seventeen cat mummies.

'It depended,' said Topher. 'They did go in for cat sacrifice, you know.'

He was in fact fed up with looking at dead things. He was fed up with the past. He wanted to go home, for tea with cakes – and Ka.

And Ka was there when they all arrived home. She was sunning herself on the pavement opposite Number 35. Next door's dog was inside, throwing itself at the window in a frenzy of barking. Ka was ignoring it, seemed to be contemplating a small yellow flower which had pushed its way through the tarmac. And Topher remembered the afternoon he'd gone out to look for her and seen the workmen resurfacing the path, pouring thick black tar on flowers like those, flattening them with a heavy roller. But this one had come through. And so had he. He picked Ka up and she put her paws round his neck, purring ecstatically.